Praise for Ann W

C000127330

Dreams f

Indie Next Generation Book Awards Finalist

...incredibly vivid and emotional tale of love and loyalty, friendship, loss, and faith...*Booklist*

...a lovely story about life changes and love lost and found. *Romantic Times Book Review*

Stunning! Juli Townsend, Author of *Absent Children*

Absence of Grace

...a riveting read of personal struggle, very much recommended. *The Midwest Book Review.*

Both a coming of age and a romance novel, this story is captivating and charming. But be prepared, you may not want to put it down once you start. Karen Bryant Doering, author of *Parents' Little Black Book*

...the writing is perfect. Absolutely smooth and divine. Like the best bar of chocolate. Fran Macilvey, author of *Trapped*

Counterpointe

Endorsed by Compulsion Reads

...a powerful novel of two lovers who face profound challenges. Poignant and insightful...a compelling dramatic evaluation of what it means to love or be loved. *The Midwest Book Review*

...a wonderful exploration of two people from different worlds coming together and finding love and building a lasting, realistic relationship with all the complexities, joys and sorrows that entails. *Long and Short of it Reviews*

Ann's brilliant, well–thought–out prose lifts her stories to a higher literary level than most of today's fare...prepare to be impressed. Pam Berehulke, Bulletproof Editing

Love and Other Acts of Courage

Love and Other Acts of Courage is...beautiful. The plot is engaging and it focused on the development of the characters...and the ending (is) very satisfying. Lorena Sanqui for Readers' Favorite

...a love story woven within an engaging mystery with twists and turns, believable villains, and enough tension to keep you turning pages. Dete Meserve, author of *Good Sam*

...the characterizations of Max, Jake, and Sophie are done so delicately, so perfectly, that each alone would be worthy of a separate story. In short, Love and Other Acts of Courage is so much more than a love story. Kate Moretti, NY Times bestselling author of *Thought I Knew You*

Memory Lessons

...you don't want to miss this inspirational story. David Johnson, author of *The Tucker Series*

...a real treat if you like to read novels that make you feel. Margaret Johnson, author of *The Goddess Workshop*

...high-stakes drama with real characters and an understanding of how women process memory and guilt. Patricia Macauliffe

A lovely and compelling story. Michelle Lam, author of *The Accidental Prophetess*

THE BABBLING BROOK NAKED POKER CLUB

Book Six

by

ANN WARNER

The Babbling Brook Naked Poker Club –
Book Six

Copyright © 2021 Ann Warner

Library of Congress Registration TXu-2-281-053

ISBN: 9798498153254

Edited by

Lynda Dietz – Easy Reader Editing

Cover design by

Kit Foster Design

Dedication

To my husband who keeps me feeling young

And to all the wonderful "older" women in my life who have shown me what it means to age gracefully: my mother, Evelyn,

my grandmothers, Magdalen and Myrtle,

and my aunts Josephine and Beth

Book Description

It's the holiday season, but someone is playing the Grinch at the Brookside Retirement Community. Hurtful rumors circulate about Josephine's best friends, altering the mood from joyous to troubled. Then even more disturbing events are brought to the attention of Josephine and Lill. Once again their mystery solving skills are called upon to stop the rumors and to save their fellow residents from a pair of determined scam artists.

Chapter One

Josephine

"I met an interesting new resident today," Norman told me as we sat down to dinner. Meeting new residents is a regular thing for Norman these days. He's a very social man. In fact, for a short time, he was the Brookside Retirement Community's activities director. Actually, he was undercover, investigating stolen art, but the activities director job suited him, and I think he misses it. Now he makes up for that by serving on the welcoming committee for new Brookside residents.

"One Glorious Pennycutt," he said.

"My goodness." I blinked, trying to come up with a vision to match such an evocative name. "Stately, silken curls, ruby lips, and . . . perhaps a feather boa?"

"Not exactly."

"Well?"

"For starters, she's roughly this tall." Norman's hand rested mid-chest, eliminating "stately" from the description. "Short hair and, like you, she doesn't wear lipstick, so yes to curls, but no to ruby lips. Oh, and she's roughly this wide." He held his arms out. "A lovely, jolly dumpling of a woman."

I gave my husband of a year a startled look.

"You did nail the flowing garments, however."

"That sounds like an almost spot-on description of Myrtle Grabinowitz then. Except for the lipstick and the jolly parts." Myrtle, a former almost beauty queen who makes sure you know it within five minutes of meeting her, is no longer what one could call svelte, and she's not what I would call jolly, but she does favor fluttery garments and never leaves her apartment without having her face "on."

"While they might share a certain, hmm, aesthetic, Glorious is no Myrtle. Or vice versa."

"Norman Neuman, if I didn't know better, I might think you were smitten."

"Actually, I think maybe I am." He glanced at me with a twinkle in his eye.

Since the woman he'd just described was my polar opposite in both her physical appearance and her emotional attributes, the twinkle reassured me.

"Should I be worried?"

His lips twitched. "Possibly." Then he reached out and took one of my hands in his. "Of course not, Jo. I think you'll like her."

"Is there a Mr. Pennycutt?"

"Doesn't seem to be."

"Widowed?"

"Unclear. I've invited her to dinner next week, so you can suss out all the gory details then."

"Maybe we could include Lill?" Since Norman does most of the cooking, I defer to him on how many guests we're going to have.

"Of course."

"What about Philippa, Richard, and Edna?"

"A full table, then," Norman said.

"Only seven."

"Is that bad luck? If it is, we can round off the numbers with Myrtle."

"I'd rather not," although Myrtle does tend to sniff out get-togethers and then sometimes shows up without an invitation. But from Norman's description of Glorious Pennycutt, I think Myrtle would immediately see her as competition, and the interaction would go downhill from there, and I didn't want that to happen.

I liked the sound of Glorious, and I wanted to form an opinion of her personality without the kind of interference Myrtle would bring to the table, so to speak.

"I have another idea for evening out the numbers," Norman said. "We can invite Susannah Rasmussen."

"Who is Susannah Rasmussen?"

"She's the new resident I met earlier this

week."

"You didn't mention her."

Norman frowned and then did a quick head shake. "I thought I did."

"No. I'm quite sure you didn't." We haven't been married long enough to begin ignoring each other. "I take it, not a lovely, jolly dumpling of a woman?"

"Definitely not. She's quite thin, actually. Very . . . elegant." He frowned, sounding surprised at his words.

Interesting. "Is she witty?"

"Intelligent, I think. But I don't know if I'd call her witty."

"Well, now you've piqued my curiosity. We have to invite her." And meeting two new people might be just the thing to enliven our lives. Things have been just the tiniest bit dull since we solved the mystery of Maddie's birth family and Lill and Maddie's kidnapper has been arrested.

We need an adventure, and who better to provide it than someone new, although it's likely Glorious and Susannah will turn out to be your garden variety retirees who are mostly interested in bridge or maybe golf, the latest Netflix series or Judge Judy, and whose main physical activity will be running around imposing pictures of their grandchildren on all and sundry.

Still, it was worth a dinner party to check out their potential.

Chapter Two

Lillian

Going to Josephine and Norman's for dinner is always a treat, because Norman's cooking is exceptional and it's a chance to give one of my hats an outing. In addition, tonight we'll be meeting a new resident Norman has described as a jolly, witty dumpling. That's intrigued both Josephine and me, and we do love our intrigues.

Philippa and Richard drove Edna and me to the party. The four of us have apartments in the main Brookside building, but Josephine and Norman recently moved into one of the new standalone houses being added to the complex. Philippa and Richard would normally have walked, but since Edna and I are within hailing distance of our eighty-fifth birthdays, we always appreciate a lift.

Richard dropped us off at the front door and then parked around the corner. Josephine welcomed us, and by the time Richard arrived from parking the car, Norman was walking in from the garage with the two other guests.

Josephine, who was helping me with my coat, froze and stared at the woman who clearly wasn't a jolly dumpling with an odd expression on her face.

"Susannah Hawkins?" she said, with a shake of her head.

"It's Rasmussen now," the one named Susannah said with a slight lift of her chin. She stared back at Josephine. "Oh, my goodness. It's you, isn't it? Josephine Bartlett. Why I haven't seen you in . . . what has it been? Thirty years, at least. Maybe forty. This is a surprise."

"It's Neuman now," Josephine said in a prim tone I haven't heard her use in ages.

"Indeed. So this lovely, lovely man is married to you. I never would have guessed." She tipped her head toward Norman with a cat-in-the-cream smile that hinted at secret assignations, something I knew was impossible, and I knew that Josephine also knew.

Despite that, Josephine's response made it clear the presence of Susannah Hawkins, now Rasmussen, was both surprising and unwelcome. Seeing Josephine struggling to come up with a response to the comment about Norman, I stepped toward Susannah and offered my hand as a distraction.

"My name's Lillian Fitzel. Welcome to Brookside."

"Oh, yes. Why thank you. Oh, I like your hat."

I was wearing one of what Josephine calls my

beanie hats as opposed to what I wear to church. Those she calls my Kentucky Derby hats. This beanie is navy with a pink rose, forget-me-nots, and a tiny veil, and is one of my favorites for evening wear.

We milled around as coats were collected and names were exchanged. Then Josephine led the way into the living room, and Norman followed with a tray of drinks. While he distributed glasses of wine, I turned to Glorious.

"What a wonderful name you have." Although we'd so far only exchanged greetings, I could already see exactly why Norman had described Glorious the way he had. If I were able to detect auras, I do believe hers would be a bright magenta with sparkles.

On the other hand, I'd guess Susannah's would be an angry red with dark streaks, although that didn't make a lick of sense.

"Lill's right. You do have an unusual name," Josephine said, following my lead. She'd waited for everyone to choose a seat before sitting as far from Susannah as she could manage.

"Oh my, yes I do. You can call me Glory, by the way."

"Did you get teased at school?" I was a teacher, so I know that unusual names are magnets for bullies.

"No, but that's only because at that time I was just plain Doris Davis." She scrunched her nose, looking even more appealing. "When I went out into the world on my own, I decided to celebrate my new life with a new name."

"What a very peculiar thing to do," Susannah said.

"I don't think so," Glory said, turning to Susannah with a wide smile. "After all, it appears that both you and Josephine have changed your names along the way as well."

"Because I got married. And I didn't change my entire name."

Glory shrugged. "Different strokes and all that. But I have to say it's been one of the best things I've done."

"That sounds like a story," Philippa said.

"Philippa's a novelist, so she collects stories," Josephine said.

I was glad to see Josephine gradually emerging from her initial startled reaction to Susannah's presence.

"And may I say, I sure never dreamed I'd be able to afford to retire to a place like this," Glory said, ignoring the request for the story about her name.

"Oh, neither did I," Edna said. "Although, the truth is, if it wasn't for the benevolent fund, I'd be living in my son's basement."

Edna doesn't know it, but Josephine is the one who set up the fund that helps Brookside residents like her stay on after they've run out of money. In fact, Josephine designated Edna as the first recipient, even though it was after we discovered Edna was a thief. She's now reformed and is a model Brookside resident and a good friend, something none of us would have predicted not that long ago.

"So how do you afford it?" Susannah asked Glory.

I thought it extremely poor manners to ask such a question, even if Glory had introduced the subject.

Glory waved her almost empty wine glass and shrugged her shoulders. "An unexpected inheritance."

"From whom?" Susannah said.

I was quite interested in the response, but I doubted any of the rest of us would have asked the question. Although Susannah had contributed only a few words to the conversation, I'd already decided she wasn't someone I wanted to get to know better, even without Josephine's reaction to go by.

I exchanged a glance with Josephine, who rolled her eyes. I translated easily. It was her "we'll talk later," eye roll.

"How about you?" Glory said, facing Susannah and ignoring the question about the source of the inheritance. "How did you pick Brookside?"

"Oh, well, I know several residents, and they speak highly of it. And after my husband passed, well, I just didn't have any interest in keeping such a large house. And my sons were very supportive of my moving here. They're both extremely successful with large homes of their own, so neither of them wanted the house. That reminds me, how is your son, Josephine?"

As Josephine's friends, we know not to mention her son. It's a complicated story, but suffice it to say, as a result of what happened, not one of us ever mentions Jeff to her.

After a pause, Josephine said, "He's fine. And it's nice to hear your sons are doing well." The prim tone was back.

"Oh, they are. Wonderfully well. Both my sons married lovely women and they've given me three gorgeous granddaughters and a grandson who are all smart as whips."

It felt to me like Susannah had just picked up a muddy rag and was busily rubbing Josephine's face with it, and I wanted to slap her for it. I had no idea how we were going to get through an entire meal with this woman.

"Josephine, I just have to say, you have the most elegant home," Glory said. "And there has to be a story behind that painting." She gestured toward the painting hanging on the wall behind Susannah, who twisted around to look.

I thought it was lovely of Glory to take over and change the subject like that, since the rest of us had been rendered briefly mute by Susannah's astonishing pushiness. And commenting on the painting was perfect, since there is a rather nice story behind it. But perhaps not one to be shared with the likes of Susannah.

The painting is of a woman and a young girl facing each other in a stubbled wheat field. It's a peculiar but intriguing image that brings to mind Andrew Wyeth's *Christina's World*. Maddie painted it and gave it to Josephine as a thank you.

A timer went off, and Norman stood. "That's reminding me it's time I dished up," he said, effectively shutting off the subject of the painting.

"Oh, let me help," Philippa said, jumping to her feet and following Norman from the room.

That left Josephine to lead the way to the dining room, where she assigned us seats at the table, placing Glory and me next to her at one end and Susannah and Edna at the other end next to Norman. Philippa and Richard took the middle seats. As we ate, Josephine and Norman, with the rest of us helping, managed to steer the conversation into general channels. Until the very end, when Susannah once again brought up

Josephine's son.

"You must tell me all about Jeff," Susannah said. "Where does he live and what is he doing now?"

"No doubt eating dinner," Josephine said, setting her fork down.

Susannah tittered. "Of course he is. But I mean, what's his career? And do you have grandchildren?"

I desperately searched my mind for a way to stop or deflect the questions. Philippa looked like she was doing the same thing.

Josephine lifted her chin and stared at Susannah. "He's a financial planner, he lives in Cincinnati, and he never had children." Her words were devoid of the emotion I knew she had to be feeling.

"Oh, that *is* too bad," Susannah said, looking, to my eyes, more delighted than sympathetic. "Grandchildren are such a blessing, you know."

"Well, of course, they can be," Glory said, looking from Susannah to Josephine. "But one can't be too self-satisfied about such things. Not every sweet grandchild turns out to be a blessing."

"You must not have any," Susannah said, her attention briefly pulled from Josephine to Glory.

"Not yet, I'm sorry to say. But I have enough experience to know there are no guarantees that every grandchild will grow into a delightful adult."

Norman stood and picked up his plate. "Is everyone finished?"

"It was delicious," Glory said, turning a wide smile on Norman, and leaving Susannah and her glare in the lurch. Glory gathered up her plate and Richard's to hand to Norman.

"I hope you don't mind," Philippa said, turning to Josephine. "But we need to get back by seven. We're expecting an important call."

That was more than a little weird since both Philippa and Richard have cell phones, but seeing the look of relief on Josephine's face, I understood what Philippa was doing.

"Oh, that's good, because it fits right into Edna's and my plans," I said, smiling at Philippa. I could see Edna opening her mouth, no doubt to say, "What plans." I wasn't close enough to kick her, so I talked over her instead.

"There's a concert at seven. You should come." I aimed the last comment at Glory and Susannah.

"I'd completely forgotten about the concert," Glory said. "I hope you don't mind taking us back for it?" she asked Norman.

He smiled and said of course he didn't mind.

On that note, the dinner party came to an abrupt but extremely welcome conclusion.

"Wow. Wasn't that something," Philippa said as we drove back to the main building.

"It's obvious there's history there," was Richard's contribution.

"Do you think Josephine will want to talk about it?" Philippa asked as Richard stopped by the front door to let us out.

"Maybe let her decide," I said.

"I suppose," Philippa said.

But although I was the one suggesting we wait for Josephine to tell us what was going on, my personal plan was to call first thing in the morning and ask Josephine all about Susannah Hawkins, now Rasmussen.

Chapter Three

Josephine

Norman had left me in the kitchen while he drove Glory and Susannah back to the main building. When he returned, I was still standing in the same place, lost in memory.

"You okay, Jo?"

"Of course."

"So, what's going on?"

"You're absolutely right, you know. Glory is lovely. And dinner was delicious."

He set his keys down and frowned at me. "I do hope you realize that while I may be getting older, I can still notice you're not answering a question I asked you ten seconds ago."

I sighed. "We'd better sit down." I led the way to the living room, and Norman turned on a lamp.

He sat next to me on the sofa and took one of my hands in his. "I could tell you didn't like Susannah much. And for that matter, I confess neither did I."

"Do you think anyone else noticed?"

"The only one who possibly didn't was Edna. So, tell me, how do you know her?"

"One of her wonderfully successful sons is the same age as Jeff, and the other is a year younger."

"And?"

"So, she knew me. Who I was, who I was married to. And one day in New York . . ."

"Ahh, she saw you with Daniel," Norman said after it was clear the words were stuck in my throat.

Norman is both intuitive and has had years of experience fitting tiny clues into logical narratives, but since neither of us has mentioned Daniel since I told Norman the story early in our relationship, I was startled that he'd figured it out so quickly. Daniel was the man I bought my Edward Hopper painting from, fell in love with, and then visited twice a year for over fifteen years.

"Susannah was in New York for a weekend of theater. She saw us at a play, and later she made sure I knew she'd seen us."

I considered that sighting solid proof that Murphy and his law were in firm control of the universe. Especially since I only went to New York to see Daniel when Thomas had a weekend golf outing or was on an extended business trip. And given I'd been over seven hundred miles from home, I shouldn't have had to worry about running into someone I knew.

"Susannah's husband and Thomas were executives at the same bank. She sidled up to me at the obligatory Christmas party that year, gave me an arch look, and asked me what I'd thought of *Kiss of the Spider Woman*. I knew it wouldn't do any good to try to convince her the man she'd seen me with was a relative or an old friend, so I didn't try. I simply started to walk away from her. She grabbed my arm and told me she'd be happy to keep my trips to New York and my *special friend* a secret if I made it worth her while." I pulled my hand free of Norman's and rubbed my forehead.

"Did you? Make it worth her while?"

"I asked what it would take, and she said the next time I was in New York I could pick her up a Gucci handbag."

"Expensive, I take it?"

"Very."

"Did you? Get the handbag for her?"

"No. I don't like bullies or blackmailers. Besides, I didn't think one handbag would end it."

"So what happened?"

"It was odd. Nothing happened. I think in my heart of hearts I hoped she would say something. Because if Thomas believed her and confronted me, it might have given me the courage to end the marriage. But he never said anything, so either she didn't tell him, or he didn't care."

I stopped to gather my thoughts and catch my breath.

"Jeff graduated the next spring, so I was no longer attending any school functions where I might run into Susannah, and that next Christmas, I faked an illness, so I didn't have to go to the party. And that was that. Until tonight."

"I'm sorry I invited her."

"There was no way you could've known."

"Well, now at least we'll know to avoid her."

"Indeed we will."

Still, it was bad luck that a woman I disliked so heartily had chosen to move into the retirement community where I was living. Murphy obviously had a warped sense of how best to use his power.

Chapter Four

Lillian

I ran into Glory on the way in to lunch, and we decided to sit together. We'd just settled our napkins on our laps when Susannah walked up to us.

"How nice to see you both again. May I join you?"

We had no choice but to smile and nod.

"Tu la ru, Lillian, and these must be our newest residents. How delightful. I'm Myrtle Grabinowitz. I do apologize for missing your orientation session. I've been so looking forward to meeting you both. Lillian, how did you get the jump on me?" Without waiting for an answer or asking permission to join us, Myrtle abandoned her walker, pulled out the fourth chair, and plopped into it, fanning her face with a tissue.

"Is it just me, or is it warm in here?"

Being well acquainted with Myrtle's sudden

segues, I ignored the question and simply handed her the menu card sitting by my plate to use as a fan. The table Glory and I had chosen had only two place settings, but that hadn't deterred either Susannah or Myrtle from sitting down.

"Now, I know one of you is Susannah and the other is Glorious. And may I just say, that's certainly an unusual name."

"I'm Susannah." She reached out a slender hand, and she and Myrtle shook hands, their expressions ones of mutual satisfaction.

"So that means you're Glorious," Myrtle said.

"Please, call me Glory."

"Oh, yes. I much prefer that. Glorious is such a peculiar name. Why did your parents choose it? Is it a family name?"

"She picked it for herself," Susannah said. "In fact, I'm not sure you ever finished the story about that, but perhaps we were all distracted by Norman's cooking. I must say, that was a surprise. For such a masculine man to do the cooking while his wife sits back and gets waited on hand and foot."

"Josephine does not sit back and let Norman wait on her." The words popped out before I had a chance to think about what I was saying or who I was saying it in front of.

"Wait. You've met Josephine and Norman?"

Myrtle said. "When was this?"

"Why, last night," Susannah said. "Norman invited us for dinner so we could meet other people."

By the time Susannah finished that statement, Myrtle was staring at me with a deeply wounded expression. "Other people? And you were one of them, Lillian?"

"Oh, yes," Susannah said. "And so were Philippa, Richard, and Edna, wasn't it? It was quite a jolly party."

Myrtle's lips twitched. "No doubt."

I flipped through several possible things to say to ease Myrtle's hurt feelings, but I was afraid all of them would simply add to her distress.

"And now here we four are with an opportunity to get better acquainted," Glory said. "Why don't we go around the table and tell each other something interesting about ourselves."

Myrtle sniffed and gave Glory a stiff nod.

"I'll start, shall I?" Glory said. "You asked about my name. Well, when I left home I decided that since I was beginning a new life, I should change my name to something distinctive and memorable."

"You certainly managed that," Susannah said.

"However did you come up with Glorious and Pennycutt?" Myrtle asked, her ruffled feathers beginning to smooth out.

"I went to the library and looked at obituaries in the local paper. The very first day, I found the name Pennycutt. Then I had to decide on a first name, but I struggled with that until a couple of days later. What happened was this. As I was leaving the library, one of the librarians smiled and said something about wasn't it a perfectly glorious day. And that was that. Glorious Day Pennycutt."

"Weren't your friends and family confused when you did that?" Myrtle asked.

"My parents died when I was young, and I was raised by a great-aunt who smoked and swore at a time when it was rare for a woman to do so. She was very supportive." She grinned at us. "So who wants to be next?" she said.

"I'll go," Myrtle said. "Let's see. I have five children. Two boys and three girls, eleven grandchildren and four great-grandchildren."

"My goodness," Susannah said. "That's quite a brood."

"Accomplishment," Glory said, overlapping Susannah's word.

"Do you have children, Glory?" Myrtle said, ignoring Susannah.

"A daughter. But she lives in France, so I don't get to see her often."

"That's a shame," Myrtle said. "I don't know

what I'd do if I didn't get to see my children all the time. And, oh, yes. I forgot to say I was also president of the PTA for many years, and I organized several of the school fundraisers."

"My, you've had a useful and eventful life," Glory said.

"Indeed I have," Myrtle said, sitting back and folding her arms with a look of satisfaction.

I was surprised that Myrtle hadn't included the fact she was almost Miss America in her narrative. That has always seemed to be the accomplishment she's most proud of. Or at least the one she talks about the most. But I had no idea she'd been a PTA president. That can be such a thankless job. She did say one time that she'd raised money in the past, but I pictured her as a Girl Scout den mother, or something of the sort.

"Lillian, do you want to go next?" Glory seemed to have effortlessly taken over as our leader, and may I just say it was a huge relief.

"My husband and I were married fifty-five years. We were both teachers, and we had two daughters, each of whom has a daughter. After I retired, I became a certified handwriting analyst and consulted with a large company headquartered in Cincinnati to help them choose their executives."

"Let me guess," Susannah said. "P&G?"

"Close," I said. I never tell anyone exactly

which company.

"GE?" Susannah said, still guessing. I was beginning to notice that Susannah can be quite insistent about all sorts of details.

"You probably had to sign a confidentiality agreement," Glory said.

"Oh, yes. I certainly did." I smiled at her. I was beginning to like Glory Day Pennycutt very much.

"What about you, Susannah? What should we know about you?" Glory said.

"I have two sons who are very successful businessmen who are married to lovely women, and they all spoil me rotten."

I thought it interesting there was so little information about what she'd done with her life.

"Oh, and the way I know Josephine is that my sons were in school with her son. We'd lost touch, though, so it's thrilling to find her again."

Thrilling? Not the word Josephine would use. I'd talked to her this morning, and she'd told me how and when she'd known Susannah and about Susannah's threatening her. It wasn't something I wanted to hash out in front of Myrtle, however, although I would have loved to have said something like, "You mean after you tried to blackmail her?"

"Have you met her son?" Susannah directed

the question to Myrtle and me.

"Oh, we have, haven't we, Lillian?" Myrtle said with a titter. "But he never visits. I think there may even be a restraining order involved."

"How odd," Susannah said, looking, to my eyes, rather delighted.

"There was a bit of a fuss. Over the painting, wasn't it?" Myrtle said, turning to me with a frown of concentration.

There have been hints lately that Myrtle's memory is slipping, but this was a strong indication it hasn't slipped entirely. I debated about how much to say in front of Susannah, who I suspected would jump on any negative information about Josephine she could find. There was a sly edge to almost everything she said about Josephine. So, I needed to counter that restraining order comment.

"You're mixing him up with Eddie," I told Myrtle. It was a blatant attempt on my part to divert Myrtle's thoughts from Josephine's son to a man who had been an aide here at Brookside. And a thoroughly nasty piece of work he was.

"Yes, of course you're right, Lillian. How could I possibly forget Eddie?"

"Long story," I told the other two.

"So. Josephine's son. He doesn't visit at all?" Susannah said. I tell you, she was as determined as a shark going after a seal.

"No, they don't get along," Myrtle said.

Thank goodness she'd dropped the restraining order memory.

"How sad," Susannah said, and I swear she was smirking.

I glanced across at Glory.

"Well, I don't know about the rest of you, but I'm starving," Glory said, catching my eye.

While we'd been chatting, the staff had set places for Susannah and Myrtle and had delivered our drinks and salads. With Myrtle's attention turning to food, the subject of Josephine's son was thankfully dropped.

After lunch, Glory and I excused ourselves at the same time and walked out together, leaving Susannah, no doubt, to continue to pump Myrtle for information. I'd have to let Josephine know.

"A witch on a bike, that one," Glory said, leaning toward me as we walked out of the room.

"Susannah, you mean?"

"Of course. Myrtle, on the other hand, is interesting. She seemed quite upset about the dinner party."

"Oh, she was, unfortunately. Perhaps you'd like to come to my place for a cup of tea, and I can fill you in?"

"I'd love it," Glory said with a smile.

I prepared a pot of one of the exotic teas Josephine regularly gifts me with and put out a plate of cookies.

"I shouldn't," Glory said, taking a cookie. "But you can probably tell I have a weakness for sweets, and chocolate chip cookies are my favorite. However, I'd appreciate it if you'd put the rest out of reach."

"Certainly." I picked up the plate and returned it to the kitchen. "I want to thank you for the way you handled both Susannah and Myrtle at lunch," I said, sitting back down.

"It did feel like things were about to go sideways," Glory said with a smile. "So, let's see. You were going to tell me about Myrtle?"

"Oh, dear, where to begin? Well, she has a really good heart, something I'm not at all sure I can say about Susannah."

"I think we can say with some certainty that we can't say that about Susannah," Glory said.

We laughed together.

"Let's see, what else? Well, Myrtle has an amazing talent for sticking her nose into other people's business, especially Josephine's and mine, at critical points and then coming up with bizarre but often nearly correct explanations for what she's seen or heard."

"Perhaps she honed that talent as a mother of five."

"You know, you could be right about that."

"So you're saying you and Josephine have had

business that Myrtle's inserted herself into at critical moments?"

"It was a minor miracle she didn't sniff out the dinner party last night and show up on the doorstep."

"That would have been impressive."

"It is. Somehow she always manages to find someone to drive her over whenever she suspects something interesting is happening."

"But, you say she has a good heart."

"She does. Just don't share anything with her you don't want everyone living in or visiting Brookside to know."

"Got it. What about Susannah?"

"I think your initial impression was the correct one." I didn't think it was my place to tell Glory the whole story that Josephine had told me this morning. Better to leave it up to Josephine whether to share.

Glory nodded and took a sip of tea. "I'm thinking she might be a good person to avoid."

"Good luck with that. She seems to have decided we're her new best friends."

Glory gave me a rueful look. "You have any suggestions?"

"Arrive late for meals, so you're the one choosing where to sit."

"I suppose that's better than telling her to go

fry ice."

"My goodness, I haven't heard that expression in years. My husband used to say that."

"Why, so did mine," Glory said.

We sipped tea in silence for a time. I didn't know about her, but I was thinking how lovely it would be if Roger could walk through the door and join us. He didn't like tea, but I would have jumped up immediately and made him a cup of coffee.

"So, about Josephine's son. Any idea why Susannah keeps bringing him up?"

"Clearly so she can lord it over Josephine with her oh-so-successful sons."

"Josephine's son isn't successful?"

"I don't actually know."

"And the painting. What was that about?"

"Josephine owns an Edward Hopper painting. *Sea Watchers*. She had it hanging on her living room wall, and when her son saw it he made such a fuss she couldn't keep it here. And then he tried to get Josephine declared incompetent so he could get his hands on it."

"My goodness. Didn't Norman have something to say about that?"

"This was before they were married."

Glory sat back, sipping her tea, apparently going over what I'd told her. Nothing that was private, of course.

"And the Eddie person you mentioned?"

"He broke into Josephine's apartment and hid the painting under her bed so he and Edna could collect a ransom for revealing the hiding place." I dislike gossip, but all of this was factual and widely known by any number of people.

Glory sat back, blinking rapidly. "You're talking about the Edna we met last night?"

"Indeed. Edna almost made it to master criminal status with that caper. She's since reformed, and even though what she did is common knowledge, please don't say anything to her."

"Of course not. My word, I certainly never expected such excitement when I moved here."

"It was probably exactly as boring as you expected it to be before Josephine and her painting arrived. But she and I have since had several adventures. Unfortunately, I fear that's all behind us now."

Glory looked at me over the rim of her cup and raised her eyebrows in question.

"It would take much too long to tell you everything," I said.

She continued to stare at me so I gave her a quick summary of our involvement in the return of artwork worth hundreds of millions of dollars to the Elizabeth Kent Oakes Museum in Boston.

And the unmasking of a murderer years after she'd done the deed. Glory gave me an odd look, and I realized I was beginning to sound like a deranged old lady with delusions of grandeur. I stopped speaking and took a breath. "I know. It's all pretty unbelievable. I think you better ask Josephine for the rest of the details."

Glory cocked her head and gave me an assessing look. "I believe you, but I'm definitely going to have to talk to Josephine if that's the best way to get the rest of the story."

"It is," I said.

Chapter Five

Devi

I'd just gotten off the phone with Josephine, who'd called to make a date for lunch, when Mac arrived home. The twins gave him their usual rapturous welcome, and then it was my turn. He kissed me, but he seemed distracted, and I wondered if he was worried about something. But asking about it, whatever *it* might be, was a nonstarter with Lily and Toby still up and around. They're nearly two and since there are two of them, they keep us hopping. We save serious talks for after they're in bed.

Mac went off to lock up his gun and change clothes while I got the twins into their high chairs and began the process of feeding them. Lily's easy, but Toby is super finicky, so it always helps when Mac joins in and takes one twin while I take the other.

"Is something wrong?" I was getting a definite vibe and no longer wanted to wait until bedtime. Since the twins were strapped into their high chairs, we could afford to turn part of our attention away from them.

He didn't look at me as he offered Lily her next bite. "Lisa called today."

Lisa is Mac's ex-wife and the twins' biological mother. She's caused us a fair amount of drama, so it's a relief that she and her second husband, Nick, are currently in Japan, and will be for another two years.

"And?" I said, recovering a dollop of squash before it dripped off Toby's chin.

"She's coming for a visit. She and the baby. Next week."

Lisa and Mac had so much trouble conceiving, Lily and Toby are the result of *in vitro* fertilization. But then Lisa got pregnant the usual way a few months after she and Nick got married.

"Did she have a boy or a girl?" I had to ask, since we hadn't heard from Lisa in months.

"Girl. She asked if she could stay with us."

That announcement put an abrupt halt to my nudging at Toby to take another bite. "What did you tell her?" He couldn't very well say we don't have room since we're living in a house with seven bedrooms.

"She took me by surprise, I'm afraid. I said I'd let her know."

"That's as good as admitting we have the room."

"I know. Not my finest moment."

"I suppose she expects us to pick her up at the airport as well?"

Mac sighed. Lily gurgled at him, and he smiled at her. "I don't think it's a good idea for her to rent a car after such a long flight."

I remember how exhausted I was after flying back from Japan with the twins and what a relief it had been to know that Mac would be waiting for me.

"She could take a shuttle."

Mac wasn't meeting my gaze.

"So what did you commit to?"

Mac finds it difficult to say no to Lisa. I can't very well take him to task for it, because I'm not much better. It's a long, complicated story, but if it hadn't been for Lisa having the embryos secretly implanted after she and Mac divorced, we wouldn't have the twins, since I can't have children after being shot. Bottom line, we owe her a ginormous debt of gratitude. Although that doesn't mean either of us chooses to be in her company if we can help it.

"Oh, all right," I said. "I'll pick her up." Since I work near downtown Cincinnati, and Lisa's flight would arrive in the late afternoon, that made the most sense.

"I can book her a hotel, if you don't want her here," Mac said, wiping Lily's face and lifting her out of the highchair.

"You know she'll want to spend time with the twins, and the minute she sees this house, she'll start making snarky comments about staying here. We might as well suck it up from the get-go."

"Have I ever told you how amazing you are, Mrs. McElroy?" Mac said, dropping a kiss on the top of my head.

"I think I remember hearing it a time or two," I said. "And, for your information, I never get tired of hearing it. I guess we could put her in the blue bedroom." It's the farthest one from our room, so if the baby isn't sleeping through the night, we won't know about it. Although, no matter where in the house we put Lisa, just having her nearby was going to be a trial.

~ ~ ~

I waited in the airport pickup area where Mac had waited for me and the twins when we returned from Japan. Lisa had connected through Minneapolis, like I had, so I knew I wouldn't have to wait long after her flight's arrival for her to arrive at the main terminal.

Passengers streamed by, but then I saw Lisa. She was pushing a stroller, but oddly, she didn't seem to have any other luggage. We'd be picking up her checked baggage upstairs, but traveling with a baby would be impossible without at least a diaper bag.

As she exited the secure area, I stepped toward her. She caught sight of me, slowed, and frowned. The woman walking behind her bumped into her, and Lisa turned and said a sharp word before continuing toward me.

"I thought Darren would be picking me up."

Lisa is the only person I know who refers to Mac by his first name.

I shook my head. "Made more sense for me to be the one to come." As I finished speaking, I noticed the woman who'd bumped Lisa was now standing behind her and had lowered a large diaper bag to the ground. While Lisa didn't look too bad, this woman, a slight, middle-aged Japanese woman, looked exhausted.

I tipped my head toward the woman and gave Lisa a questioning look.

"Oh, that's Hiroko. She's the nanny."

"Nice to meet you, Hiroko. I'm Devi."

Hiroko put her hands together and bowed. I bowed back.

"Her English isn't very good," Lisa said.

I leaned down to greet the baby, who looked back at me with wide eyes. I reached out to smooth a wisp of hair off her forehead.

"What's her name?" I asked.

"Michelle. But Hiroko insists on calling her Mika. Hadn't we better collect the luggage?"

"Yes, of course."

As we went up the escalator to baggage claim, I helped Hiroko with one of the carry-ons she'd been wrangling.

The checked luggage was already circling the carousel. That's one of the nice things about the Cincinnati airport. They do a really great job with baggage. Lisa had three large cases, and there was a smaller, more battered case that I suspected belonged to Hiroko.

"Why don't you wait here, and I'll bring the car around," I told them, after Hiroko and I had managed to move the luggage to one of the exit doors.

"I can come with you," Lisa said.

"No, that's okay. I'll make it quick."

Without giving her a chance to respond, I hurried out the door. I needed at least two minutes alone to call Mac.

"She has a nanny with her. Hiroko's her name," I told him, when he answered.

"So what's the plan?"

"She hasn't said. It's been kind of hectic getting the luggage sorted. What do you suggest I do? She said the woman's English isn't very good, and I feel kind of sorry for her."

"Who? Hiroko?"

"Yes. Lisa hangs back and lets her do all the heavy lifting."

"Oh, you mean she treats her like she treated you?"

Mac was referring to the time I accompanied Lisa to Japan to help with the twins. While she'd spent most of the fourteen-hour flight sleeping, I'd been left to take care of Lily and Toby. It looked to me like Hiroko had suffered the same fate with Mika—a name I liked better than Michelle.

"Why don't you just ask Lisa what her plans are and see what she says," Mac said.

It was as good a strategy as any.

I pulled up to the curb, and Lisa transferred Mika into the infant car seat I'd brought along. That left Hiroko and me to wrestle the luggage into the trunk. Once we were driving out of the airport, I tried Mac's suggestion.

"So, what are your plans?"

"Well, Mac did say we could stay with you."

"We were only expecting you and the baby." I kept my voice down and glanced in the mirror at Hiroko, who'd sat back with her eyes closed. She looked exhausted. I couldn't tell if she understood or was even paying attention to what we were saying.

"Well, you are doing that house-sitting thing in yet another huge house, aren't you? It shouldn't make any difference to you to have one more person. Besides, Hiroko's here to take care of Michelle."

"So how long do you plan on being here?"

"I haven't decided yet."

That made my throat tighten. She'd told Mac a "few" days, and he'd been unable to get her to replace that "few" with a number. But surely, both she and Hiroko had tickets with return dates on them, so why the reluctance to clarify matters? Wouldn't she be going back to spend the holidays with Nick in Japan?

I decided to let the subject go for the moment. Driving down the interstate at high speed is neither the best time nor the right place to have a serious conversation with your husband's ex.

"It was a good flight?" I asked, trying for bland.

"Oh, very nice. And it's such a relief to be home. You cannot imagine. I mean, Japan is okay, but it's terribly foreign, don't you think?"

I'd spent most of my short visit to Japan caring for Lily and Toby and saving Lisa's life when she'd become dangerously dehydrated from a serious bout of morning sickness. So, I'd had little chance to assess the foreignness factor. But what I had experienced had delighted me.

"How much longer is it that you and Nick have there?" I asked, thinking it was another no-drama subject to introduce. Besides, I knew the answer. Or I thought I did.

"Oh, he's still got another two years. He loves the place."

Not including herself in that statement was ominous, and suddenly I wished I hadn't been so quick to agree to her staying with us.

I waited too long to ask the follow-up. Or maybe I was too fearful of the answer, but in the next moment Lisa yawned.

"Hope you don't mind, but I think I'll get a little shut-eye." Without waiting for me to respond, she put the seat back, and soon she was breathing deeply. I glanced at Hiroko in the mirror and realized she was examining me with half-closed eyes.

I looked away. I really didn't want to test the

limits of her English proficiency while I was driving. Instead, I turned the radio on low and left the three travelers to their slumbers.

~ ~ ~

Lisa walked into the house ahead of me as if she owned the place. She'd taken Mika out of the car seat, but left the rest of the luggage for Hiroko and me to handle. Inside, the twins came running to greet me as they always did. In addition to being pretty good runners, they're beginning to talk. Or at least Lily is.

Mika started to cry.

"Here, take her," Lisa said, holding the baby out in a way that forced the issue. Then, ignoring me, Lisa greeted the twins, who were much more interested in Mika than they were in a strange adult.

"Do you think she's hungry?" I asked, trying to regain Lisa's attention.

"Probably. Hiroko will take care of it."

Hiroko and I exchanged a glance as she rummaged in the diaper bag, finally pulling out a bottle.

Mac walked into the developing chaos, and immediately the twins abandoned Mika to greet him. As they did, Lisa maneuvered me and then the twins out of the way and gave him a big smacking kiss. Mac pulled away and rolled his eyes at me over Lisa's shoulder.

"Well, Darren, aren't you going to say it's good to see me?"

I waited to see how Mac would maneuver out of that one. He did it by picking up Lily and swinging her around to delighted squeals.

"These are some digs," Lisa said, looking around. "I had no idea police chiefs were paid so well."

Neither of us responded to that since we knew she knew the house wasn't ours, that the owners were on a sabbatical.

She cocked her head and smiled at me. "I could really use a lie down. Maybe you could show me my room. Oh, and Darren, you'll take care of the luggage for me, won't you, sweetie?"

Sweetie? Mac and I exchanged another glance that involved raised brows and eye rolls.

"Come on, I'll show you." I led the way upstairs to the two bedrooms across from each other at the end of the hall.

She glanced at them and then turned to me with a pout. "I think we passed a much larger room back there."

"Possibly. But these are the rooms I prefer you use."

"What about Michelle? Where will she sleep?"

"You can make up a bed on the floor for her." I pointed at the pile of bedding I'd left on the chair. "Sorry, but we don't have an extra crib."

"Hmph. I must say, that's not very welcoming, Devi."

That was too bad, because it was as much welcome as I could manage. Five minutes in and Lisa had already managed to get on my last nerve.

"Why don't you take your nap, and we can talk further at dinner."

"Oh, okay. If that's the way you're going to be."

"I rather think it is," I said under my breath as I turned and left the room.

I went back downstairs to find Hiroko feeding Mika and the twins watching. Mac was off changing clothes, and Annie, our babysitter, had left.

"I tell her okay she leave," Hiroko said, looking up at me as I walked in.

"Oh, you speak English?"

"I do. Ma'am has trouble with understand me."

Hiroko did have a strong accent, and her peculiar phrasing meant I had to concentrate in order to understand her, but being able to communicate with her would make things easier for all of us.

"I expect you're tired," I said.

"Oh, yes. Flight very long."

"I know. I've done it. Was Mika good?"

"She always very good baby. Your babies, they very nice, too."

"They are. When you finish feeding her, will she sleep, do you think?"

"I not know. She sleep very long on plane."

"Will she be sleeping in your room?"

"Of course. That is my job."

Of course it was.

By that time, Mac had joined us. We left him to supervise Mika and the twins while I took Hiroko upstairs and showed her to her room. Lisa's door was closed, and she'd moved the extra blankets into Hiroko's room. I got out sheets for Hiroko and promised I'd wake her in a couple of hours to have something to eat.

I came back downstairs to find Mika lying in her infant seat, gurgling at the twins and clearly wide awake.

"I have a bad feeling about this, Mac," I said, taking a seat on the sofa next to him.

"Why is that, love?"

"Hiroko does speak English, and when I asked her how long they were going to be here, she said she was supposed to stay a month to help Lisa—she calls her ma'am, by the way—get settled."

"And you're thinking?"

"That Lisa isn't going back to Japan."

Before Mac and I were married, Lisa had shown up on his doorstep one winter evening, begging to stay one night. He'd let her in, and she parleyed that night into months. In the end, he was the one who finally moved.

When she married Nick, we'd both sighed in relief, but she'll never be completely out of our lives since she's Lily and Toby's biological mother. When you marry someone with exes, especially one as clingy and demanding as Lisa, you have to be prepared for complications. I sighed.

"What do you need me to do?" Mac said.

"Make sure she understands she can stay here one week only, and that's it. She can afford a hotel or an apartment."

"A hotel's not so easy with a baby," Mac said, his tone neutral.

"I'm prepared to harden my heart," although glancing at Mika who was reaching for her toes while she smiled at the twins, it wouldn't be easy.

"Of course you are," Mac said, putting an arm around me.

"You know Lisa drives me nuts."

"But you have to admit, that is one cute

baby," Mac said.

"Darn."

"About dinner. Why don't I pick up some takeout. Whatever tickles your fancy. How about Indian? Or maybe Chinese?"

~ ~ ~

"I know she's going to stay until we kick her out," I told Maddie, driving to work the next day.

Maddie occupies the mother-in-law suite in the house, and since we also work together at the Cincinnati Art Museum, we usually commute together. That means she's heard at least some of my Lisa stories and knows how much I've been dreading Lisa's arrival.

"Do you need me to move out temporarily so she can have the suite?" Maddie asked.

She's in a relationship with a wonderful man, and he's asked her to move in with him, but she hasn't yet made that decision. Or maybe she has.

"Since it has a kitchen, you wouldn't have to worry about feeding her."

"Oh, trust me. Having a kitchen wouldn't keep her out of mine."

"Why not tell her you don't want her to stay?"

"Unfortunately, she knows that, and it doesn't faze her. And right now I'd like to stop thinking about her. Can we talk about Oliver instead?" I glanced over at Maddie to find her blushing. Maddie in love is a total delight, and a bit of encouragement was all it took to get her talking about Oliver.

~ ~ ~

Maddie and I arrived home to find Mac lifting grocery bags out of his vehicle.

"What's all this?" I asked.

"Lisa needed formula and diapers."

I felt a flash of irritation, and I don't think I did a good job of hiding it.

Mac put out a hand to stop me from walking inside. "But here's the really good news. The agent I phoned this morning found a two-bedroom furnished apartment in Mason. My thought is we tell Lisa she can move in there tomorrow."

"You think she'll go for it?"

"Not giving her a choice. I'd like to think I learned from my mistake last time."

I closed my eyes, breathing in the cold air and feeling a sense of relief. Although, I wasn't going to relax completely until Lisa actually left the premises.

"I can't move into an apartment," she said, when we gathered around the kitchen table after the twins and Mika were in bed and Mac told her what the arrangement was going to be.

"Because?" Mac said.

"I don't know how long I'm staying. An apartment would involve a lease and stuff."

"This one requires only a deposit and a month-by-month commitment," Mac said.

"Well, I don't know if I'm staying a month. I might only stay three weeks. So it's much more convenient for me to stay here."

"You are not staying here for three weeks. Or even three days," Mac said. "It's either the apartment or a hotel."

"I can't stay in a hotel with a baby."

"That settles it, then. The apartment it is."

"She's behind this," Lisa said, pointing at me. I was trying to keep as low a profile as possible. I'd even tried to talk Mac into letting me give this meeting a miss, but he said it was too important for our future for me not to be there.

"You've never liked me. And you've turned Darren against me."

Mac held up a hand and, amazingly, Lisa stopped talking and turned her head to look at him rather than me.

"Devi didn't turn me against you. You did that all by yourself, Lis, before I even met Devi. And I hope you haven't forgotten that Devi saved your life?"

I hoped that didn't mean I was now responsible for it, as some cultures believe, a thought I kept to myself.

"You've changed, Darren. And definitely not for the better." She got up to leave the room, but then she stopped in the doorway and turned to face us. "Okay, here's the deal. I'm sick, okay. That's why I came back. So, I'm going to need help, and, well, you're here and you have this big house, and I just can't handle an apartment right now. Especially since Hiroko has to go back in two weeks. But definitely later, after I'm healthy again."

That would likely be an ever-moving goalpost into the future. Possibly when Mika was old enough to go off to college? And Hiroko had already told me she was staying a month.

I tried to decide if I believed the rest of what Lisa was saying. She didn't look good, but she had been really, really sick during her pregnancy and possibly hadn't yet fully recovered from the birth.

From the slight change in Mac's posture, I knew his heart had just sunk, possibly lower even than mine. Once again, Lisa had shown herself to be a master of the poor-me power play.

"What's wrong with you?" Mac asked.

"The Japanese doctors couldn't figure it out. That's why I had to come home for a full workup."

She'd just confirmed my suspicion she would drag this out as long as she could.

"What are your symptoms?" I asked, even though I knew it was probably useless to try to pin her down, not to mention it was mostly Mac's job to fight it out with her.

"Overwhelming fatigue, intermittent nausea, and dizziness. It makes it impossible for me to take care of Michelle."

As if we hadn't already figured out where she was going with this.

"So, what are you going to do when Hiroko has to leave?" Mac said.

"Can't Annie take care of Michelle along with the twins? They're siblings. It'll be good for them."

The only reason we can afford Annie rather than daycare is because, with the house-sitting, we've paid no rent since we got married.

Mac was shaking his head. "Lisa, you can't simply descend on us like this and insert yourself into our lives. You have a baby and a husband and a life of your own."

"You wouldn't throw out a sick dog or cat, and you know it, Darren McElroy. And you certainly can't throw out a baby. After all, she's your son and daughter's sister."

"Half-sister," Mac said. I knew he was

grasping at straws, and that Lisa was going to win. The tyranny of the weak. That's what this was.

"And I'm not throwing you out. I've found a perfectly nice place for you to stay."

"Says you."

"What about Nick? Is he joining you soon?"

She shook her head. "He loves it in Japan."

For a time, we three faced off. Then Mac straightened his shoulders.

"Here's the deal. We're happy to help, but you are not staying with us, Lisa. You have to make other arrangements."

"But I won't be able to live on my own. Not and take care of a baby." Her voice had risen to a wail, and tears poured out of her eyes.

I had to give her credit. She's good at this. But so I'm finding is Mac.

"I'm sorry, Lisa. But I'm going to insist that you move into the apartment. I'll help you get settled, and I'll put you in touch with services to help with cleaning and with home health visits, if that's needed. But what I won't do is let you stay here."

"What about Michelle?"

"We can have Michelle visit, occasionally, but she's your responsibility. If you need to hire someone to replace Hiroko, then that's what you'll have to do."

I could have kissed him. But maybe not right this minute.

"I'd like you to be ready in the morning. Will ten work for you?" As the chief of police, Mac can arrange his hours as needed.

Lisa glared at Mac. We were clearly at a tipping point in the negotiations, so I didn't move or make a sound. Any hint of weakness on either Mac's part or mine would doom us to being stuck with Lisa, perhaps permanently.

"Oh, suit yourself," she said.

She huffed, then stood and flounced out of the kitchen.

Mac and I looked at each other, and he reached out and squeezed my hand.

"You think we're doing the right thing?" I said. "Maybe she really is sick."

"If she's really sick, we'll do what we can to help, but I'm not letting her take over our lives. And you know she would. Give Lisa an inch, and she'll be living in our spare bedroom the rest of our lives."

It was exactly what I'd been thinking. Still, it wasn't easy to be hard-hearted, especially since there was a baby involved.

"That's what she counted on," Mac said.

"What?"

"You're thinking about Mika."

"I am."

"We need to do this, love."

"I know."

When Hiroko came downstairs an hour later to heat a bottle for Mika, I joined her in the kitchen and told her what the plan was for the next day.

"I wonder what the matter. Ma'am was crying, I think. I not want to disturb."

"Look, let me give you our number. If you need our help with anything, just give us a call, okay?"

"That will be good, I think. Sometimes Ma'am stays in her room all day."

I didn't want to think about what that meant for Mika. It was a relief knowing Hiroko would be there for at least the next month, but every time I thought about what would happen after that, it made my stomach lurch.

I should probably give Josephine a call. She always manages to reassure me about what Lisa can and cannot do when it comes to interfering in my life.

Chapter Six

Myrtle

I had the most delightful day today. That new resident, Susannah, came over and joined me at lunch. Such an attractive woman. And she dresses so nicely.

"Myrtle," she said as we finished our desserts, "you are such a fount of information. And everything you have to say is just so interesting."

Her praise almost made up for Josephine's dinner party snub. Not entirely. But mostly.

"Well, there's a lot more I could tell you. Would you maybe like to come by my place? I'll make us cups of tea."

"Why, I'd absolutely love to hear the rest of your stories."

That was music to my ears. I do love telling stories.

"I'm especially interested in the adventures you and Josephine have had," Susannah said a few minutes later. She picked up the cup of tea I'd made for her out of the last of the tea Josephine gave me for my birthday and took a sip. Since Josephine only gives the special tea she orders from her tea broker to her dearest friends, I was thrilled with the gift. Although, I have to say, recent events have led me to question my status as Josephine's friend. Not something I'll be sharing with Susannah, of course.

I pushed thoughts of tea and friendship aside and settled in to tell Susannah all my best Josephine stories—the ones about her son, and how Mac saved Devi's life when she was shot, how Norman and Josephine returned lost artwork worth millions, and last, but not least, Maddie's story.

There's no reason to leave anything out, not now that the awful man who kidnapped Lillian and Maddie is awaiting trial and has been denied bail. And anyway, none of the rest of it is a secret, either. I mean, there are loads of people who know everything that happened. And you can't really say something is secret if loads of people know about, now can you.

It took quite a while to tell Susannah everything, and as I talked, I realized what a consequential few years it's been since Josephine moved into Brookside.

I could tell Susannah was amazed at all the goings on.

"I had no idea a retirement community could be such a hotbed of excitement. And it was so kind of you to tell me all about it," she said as she was leaving. And she didn't leave until practically time for dinner.

I'm quite certain Josephine won't mind that I filled Susannah in. Not after Susannah told me her sons went to school with Josephine's son, and that she and Josephine had been great friends during those years. She said she hoped they'd be able to pick up their friendship now that they're both living at Brookside. I didn't want to discourage her, but I think Josephine already has plenty of friends. Evidence for that is my being left out of the dinner party the other night.

I closed the door on Susannah and, humming, went to change for dinner. Tonight's a bingo night, and I always wear something special for that, even though hardly anyone else bothers to dress up in the evening. It's my considered opinion that anyone who gets sloppy about their appearance is simply taking a giant leap closer to the grave. I have standards, if I do say so myself. Maybe I'll run for the opening on the resident board and see if I can't get a measure passed to address some of the sloppy dress around here. Jeans, for pity's sake. At dinner. Really, I shouldn't have to put up with it.

Norman's on the board, and I know he'll agree with me about a dress code, since he always dresses nicely. Although, since Josephine is one of our more casual dressers, she'll probably get him to vote against it. Josephine's like that.

Chapter Seven

Josephine

Devi and Mac's twins turned two the last week in October. With Lisa in the picture, they decided to keep the birthday celebration low-key—a luncheon with cake and a very few friends and even fewer packages for the twins to open.

"They're too young to understand exactly what it's all about, and I don't want to overwhelm them or get them used to expecting lots of gifts, so if you want to get them something, I'd suggest a book," she'd told me when I asked.

I considered it a sensible approach, even though I'd have loved to do more. But Devi was right. Like her, I believe too much too soon isn't good for children. That didn't keep me from making a contribution to their education fund, however.

Lill, Norman, and I were the only guests from Brookside. Mac's parents had driven in from Toledo, and I watched their interactions with Lisa with interest. The word I'd use to describe them was "wary." With good reason. I doubt Mac has shared all the difficulties he and Devi have had with Lisa, but they had to know the basics, and that was more than enough to account for their tentative approach.

"What's happening with Lisa?" I asked Devi when we were alone in the kitchen after lunch.

"She's living in the apartment Mac found for her."

"Oh, that's good."

"I was really worried we were going to be stuck indefinitely with her as a houseguest," Devi said. "She claims she's sick, but we suspect she and Nick are getting divorced."

"It could be both," I said.

"Possibly. You know we were so relieved when she got married. But here we go again. Hiroko is due to leave shortly, and we're waiting to see how that goes."

"Have you asked her directly what her plans are?"

"We've tried, but she always changes the subject. So Mac said we should just keep our distance. And we're trying to do that, although we couldn't very well exclude her today."

"Of course you couldn't."

"We're hoping she'll want to spend the holidays with Nick. In Japan."

"Fingers crossed," I told her.

"And, speaking of holidays." Devi pulled in a breath. "Mac and I want to have a big party with everyone, but only if that's okay with you. We just thought while we're still living here . . ." She ran out of words and looked at me expectantly.

"Everyone?"

"You know. All the Brookside bunch." Devi counted on her fingers. "You and Norman, Lillian, Edna, Myrtle, Philippa and Richard, along with anyone else you'd like to include."

"Don't you have any friends your age?"

"Well, Maddie's coming and bringing Oliver, of course."

"Of course."

"And I suppose we'll have to include Lisa. So that's five younger persons," Devi said, sounding glum. I assume over the inclusion of Lisa.

"It's a lovely idea. There's no way we can fit that many people at our place comfortably."

"Does that mean you're okay with us doing this? We just figured that by this time next year, we'll probably be living in a much smaller house, so it would be a shame not to take advantage while we can."

It took me a second to process that. "Oh, because the owners will be back."

"In May," Devi said.

"Then we have to have it here."

"Terrific. We'll get a tree up and do some decorating, and, well . . . I don't know why, but this year just feels special."

When I told Norman about the party, he suggested we also invite Glory. "She doesn't seem to have any family nearby."

"There may be a slight problem with that," I told him. "Myrtle's upset that Glory got the seat on the resident board instead of her." It was something I'd heard about from Myrtle even before Norman had a chance to tell me.

Norman gave me a look.

"Okay, okay," I said. "You can invite her. Myrtle will just have to deal." Although I'd be bracing myself for more hurt feelings.

"Glad you see things my way," Norman said, leaning in to give me a quick kiss.

~ ~ ~

The night of the party, we drove Lill, Edna, and Glory in our car, while Philippa and Richard were bringing Myrtle, and we arrived at Devi and Mac's right behind them. Except, it wasn't three people who exited their car. It was four. And the fourth person was Susannah. I couldn't help myself; I froze.

"What's the matter, Jo?" Norman said.

"Myrtle. She must have invited Susannah," I said.

"I heard her tell Philippa that Devi said she could bring a guest," Edna said.

"Even Bertie would have been preferable," I said. Bertie's a ninety something-year-old fossil shuffling his steady way toward his hundredth birthday. He's also a sometime beau of Myrtle's, until she took him for granted one time too many, and he shifted his attentions to another lucky lady.

"Susannah and Myrtle are thick as thieves these days," Edna said. Since reforming her ways, Edna has developed a rather peculiar sense of humor. I might have found the comment funny in other circumstances, but really, did Myrtle's plus one have to be Susannah? And why did Susannah accept the invitation, anyway?

"Don't you like Susannah?" Edna asked.

"I don't, actually."

"What's the story?"

It wasn't something I wanted to get into on Devi and Mac's doorstep.

"She's an extremely unwelcome blast from the past," I said, hoping to shut down Edna's questions.

Edna nodded. "Well, we all know what that can be like. Don't worry, Josephine. If that's how you feel, we'll make sure to keep her away from you."

"Thanks. I appreciate that."

But even with that assurance, it was with a

great deal of reluctance that I walked through the door.

We were just in time to hear a snatch of Susannah and Myrtle's conversation as they walked away from us down the hall. We'd stopped in the entryway to take off our coats.

"I know you said it was a nice house, but, my goodness, I didn't expect this."

"But you said you had a big house," Myrtle said.

"Not like this. My word, we must pay police chiefs an awful lot of money."

"Oh, it isn't . . ." The two of them turned into the living room and the words faded. I raised an eyebrow at Norman, who shrugged.

"Is something the matter?" Devi said, as I handed her my coat.

"Conference?" I said. "Kitchen?"

"So what's the story?" Devi said when we reached the relative quiet of the kitchen. Mac was there, pulling a tray of something out of one of the ovens.

"That woman with Myrtle is the evil witch from my past life," I said. "She saw me with Daniel one time and tried to blackmail me." I'd told Devi about Daniel, way back, the night we'd shared a hospital room after she was shot and I'd been drugged.

Mac didn't know about Daniel, but I saw

Devi give him a look, letting him know she'd explain later.

"Blackmail?" Mac said, transferring appetizers to a plate. "You want me to arrest her?"

He was only half joking. Ever since Mac saved my life, he's been very protective.

"Unfortunately, the statute of limitations has run out," I said. "I just wanted you to know what we're dealing with. She can be very charming."

"Not to worry, Jo. We've got your back," Mac said.

Devi put an arm around my waist and hugged me to her. "If she even looks crosswise at you, I'm for kicking her into the dark of night."

"I doubt that will be necessary. But I might need you to keep me from slapping her silly."

"Now that we can definitely do," Mac said. "No silly slapping allowed."

"In return, maybe you can keep me from saying something nasty to Lisa," Devi said, glancing at Mac.

"So she's here?"

"Not my choice," Devi said. "But unavoidable."

Mac walked over and gave Devi a hug.

"She's just so . . ."

"Demanding?" Mac said.

"And she acts like she's still married to you, and that really, really bugs me."

"Don't forget, it bugs me, too. So we both have to just suck it up."

"Where are the twins?" I asked.

"Upstairs with a babysitter," Devi said. "As for us, we better get back to our guests."

"You two go ahead," Mac said. "I've got another tray to take out of the oven."

"I'll send Norman in to help. You know he loves this kitchen."

Devi and I walked into the living room. I whispered in Norman's ear that Mac needed help in the kitchen, and then we helped ourselves to glasses of wine. I stood for a moment, getting my bearings. Well, really, I was checking to see where Susannah was, so I could avoid her. She and Myrtle were talking to Edna and Philippa.

"Where's Lisa?" I asked Devi.

She sighed. "She wanted to tuck the twins in. I just hope she doesn't get them overexcited. I guess I better go check."

She put her glass of wine down and left, and I walked over to join Maddie and Oliver who were talking to Lill who was looking particularly spiffy in one of her amazing hats, this one an emerald green affair with a red poinsettia accent.

Ever since they were kidnapped together, Maddie and Lill have had a special bond. It's as unexpected a pairing, I suppose, as Devi and me, and both Lill and I feel incredibly lucky to have these two young women in our lives.

Maddie greeted me with a smile.

"Lill has been recruiting us to keep you and Cruella de Vil separated," Oliver said, leaning over to kiss me on the cheek.

He's a thoroughly lovely young man, and I'm so glad he and Maddie found each other.

I glanced over at Susannah and decided that Oliver was spot-on in calling her Cruella. All she needed to complete the look was a cigarette holder and a wreath of smoke around her head. That aside, she was straight out of central casting. Her hair, long and black with one artistic white streak, was held back by a large glittery brooch. And she was wearing a red dress that was too short and too tight for a woman in her seventh decade.

Mac and Norman arrived with fresh platters of appetizers, and Norman walked over to where Myrtle was sitting to give her first dibs. I rolled my eyes at Lill. Oliver winked at me.

"Oh, I knew I could count on you to have all my favorites," Myrtle said, accepting a small plate and filling it with mini quiches and chicken wings. Over her head, Norman gave me a look, and I had to bite my lip to stop a laugh. Norman thinks Myrtle's a hoot. For sure, she's more open about her likes, dislikes, and desires than almost anyone I've ever met. I may even envy her that openness. At least a little.

Over the next hour, groups formed and reformed, more plates of appetizers appeared and were consumed, and Christmas carols played softly in the background. I went upstairs to look in on the twins, and when I came back down, I found Susannah by herself in the den. The room was dim, lit only by the outside Christmas lights and the hallway light. She stood in partial shadow behind the rosewood desk, one arm extended.

I had the distinct impression she'd either just closed the top drawer or been about to open it.

"Can I help you with something?" I said.

She startled, but then looked up and gave me a smile that I immediately mistrusted.

"Oh, Josephine, it's you. Or do you prefer Jo? I was just looking for the bathroom."

"This isn't it."

"Of course not. But I noticed this desk. It's quite something, isn't it." She ran a finger over the inlaid design on the top that was invisible from the doorway and glanced at me. "I must say, you have very nice friends. Which is odd. I always found you so standoffish. And you remarried. I don't believe he's the man you used to visit in New York, though. Am I right?" She raised her eyebrows.

I stared at her, refusing to engage.

"So. Our Josephine, or Jo, is a real dark horse. Although maybe I should have guessed you had hidden depths when I discovered you were stepping out on Thomas. Did you know all the other moms thought he was quite delicious?"

Thomas was my first husband. The biggest mistake I ever made.

"Did you know that he and I?" She paused, giving me an intent look. "Ah, but you don't care, do you."

I knew Thomas had been unfaithful. It was only slightly surprising he'd been with Susannah. Although I was unsure I could trust her word on that since it was so clear she was determined to push my buttons, while I was equally determined she not succeed.

"Oh, come on, stop sulking, Jo. It's really quite unattractive."

That made me smile, and I almost said, "As unattractive as that dress and hairstyle make you?" But I resisted the temptation. It is the Christmas season, after all.

"About the bathroom?"

"In a minute. I like your friends, you know. But I'm having a hard time sorting everyone out."

There was an implied question, but I ignored it and waited her out.

"Yes, well. I was especially wondering about

Lisa. She's Mac's ex, but she calls him Darren. Do I have that right?"

"What difference does it make?"

"And she had twins with Mac and then remarried and had another baby? It really is quite confusing, you know."

I firmed my lips and said nothing.

"As for this house. Wow. Someone either inherited a pile or somehow made a pile. Legally, I hope."

I couldn't let that last one go by. "Devi and Mac are house-sitting."

"Oh, yes, Devi. Such a lovely young woman. Mixed race, is she? She was shot, right? As for Maddie. She's a bit intimidating, don't you think? And she really faced down a kidnapper?" She gave me an arch look that I would have loved to wipe off her face.

"I don't think you learned all that tonight."

"Some of it," she said, her finger continuing to caress the desk. "Lisa was very informative, but most of it came from Myrtle. She's quite chatty, Myrtle. But I don't know if I can believe everything she tells me. Some of it is quite fantastical."

The thought that Myrtle had blabbed everything about all of us to this woman made me so angry it was a very good thing that Devi showed up at that moment.

"Susannah was looking for the bathroom and got sidetracked," I said, trying not to clench my jaw.

"Let me show you where it is," Devi said.

I let Susannah walk past, and then I pulled the den door shut and waited in the hall for Devi to return.

"Do you keep any valuables or private papers in the desk?" I asked her.

"No, we don't use that room at all," Devi said. "Was she going through the desk?"

"I wouldn't put anything past her. I think we need to keep an eye on her."

"You go on back," Devi said. "I'll wait and make sure she doesn't wander off somewhere else."

I left Devi and went back to the party, but before taking a seat, I told Mac and Norman to keep an eye on Susannah's wanderings for the rest of the evening. Then I went and sat next to Lill.

"You were gone awhile," Lill said.

"The twins were asleep. But when I came downstairs, I found Susannah exploring."

"I wondered what was taking her so long."

"How long do you figure?"

"Mmm, maybe ten minutes."

"I don't trust her out of sight for one second," I said. "Devi and Mac better check to make sure nothing's missing."

Just then Susannah and Devi walked back in, and Susannah went over and took a seat near Myrtle. She glanced over at me, then away.

"Wow," Lill said, nodding toward Susannah. "Death ray alert."

"She just hinted that she had an affair with Thomas." Lill knows all my secrets, so she knows that although Thomas and I lived in the same house, we hadn't *lived* with each other for years before Thomas died.

"And here it's the Christmas season, goodwill to men, and women, I suppose," Lill said. "Did you know?"

"I don't know if I believe her, but it doesn't matter."

"Did you ask her if she told Thomas about you and Daniel?"

"I said as little as possible to her. Unfortunately, she's quite capable of picking up the conversational ball and running with it on her own."

"I've been watching her all evening," Lill said. "She'll engage someone in conversation, usually one of the men, and after a few sentences, I can see that person beginning to plot their escape. Except for Lisa. She and Lisa spent quite a lot of time together."

"Birds of a feather?" I said.

"I believe so."

That's the thing with Lill. She has a sharp eye, and she always picks a place to sit where she can watch everything going on. For the remainder of the party, as others came to talk to her, I moved around, joining different groups, except for the one that included Susannah. But I watched her, as I knew Lill was, ready at any moment to make sure if she left the room, one of us would follow her.

~ ~ ~

Norman arrived home from yet another resident board meeting. "I ran into Philippa afterward, and she asked if I'd heard the rumors going around about Edna and Myrtle."

"What rumors?"

"In Edna's case, someone posted a note on the bulletin board congratulating her on completing her community service after her conviction for theft."

"Who could have done such a thing? After all, what she did isn't a secret. And she's made amends, and new residents wouldn't know. That just makes me mad."

"Philippa took the note down as soon as she

saw it. But hard to know how long it had been up. As for Myrtle." Norman frowned. "It's a really odd one. Supposedly one of Myrtle's sons murdered someone and then died in prison."

"Where did Philippa pick that up?"

"She overheard Pru Parker telling one of the Frosties."

The Frosties is Norman's nickname for twin sisters whose white hair always sports colored streaks and glittery barrettes. Both are nonstop chatterers who remind me of birds, birds that keep changing the color of their plumage—red and green at the moment with Christmas coming.

"I don't think you can trust a word out of that woman's mouth," I said, meaning Pru. "She's dotty."

"But you have to admit she's right on the money with her gender identity crusade."

Norman had that right. Whenever Pru spots a man, she points at him, and in a voice that will clear blocked sinuses in a quarter-mile radius, declares, "penis." Any man who sees well enough to spot Pru before she spots him always hightails it in the opposite direction.

"So you're saying, because she can spot a man at fifty paces, she could be right about Myrtle's son?" I said.

"Not necessarily."

"I don't think she'd come up with something like that on her own. It's more likely she's repeating something someone told her. But why someone would say such a thing is beyond me. Do we even know if it's true?"

"I thought I'd check. But true or false, it seems like something a person who didn't like Myrtle would do. And the same is true for Edna," Norman said.

"And that's odd, because while I don't think Edna's that popular, everyone seems to like Myrtle, even though she can be a bit tedious at times."

"Maybe you should investigate," Norman said. "Letting rumors like that go unchallenged could poison the whole atmosphere."

It wouldn't affect us so much, since we don't live in the main residence, but Norman had a point about its potential for making things unpleasant for other residents. I called Lill to find out if she'd heard either rumor.

"About Myrtle, you say? Nope. Nary a word. And nobody's mentioned Edna to me, either."

"Well, if you do hear anything, you'll let me know?"

"Of course."

I hung up from Lill and dialed Philippa's number.

"Yes," she said, after I asked her about what Norman had told me. "I mentioned it to him because both things seemed so odd and mean-spirited. And even though Pru's an old raisin, she's not usually unkind."

"I don't know if Norman would agree with that."

"I know, I know. Richard either. I did ask Richard if he could check to see if the story about Myrtle's son was true."

"And is it?"

"One of her sons was killed in a car crash. No mention of him being suspected of murder, though. You know, Myrtle's become quite chummy with Susannah," Philippa said. "Maybe she confided in her, and the story got blown out of proportion. Like that game of telephone we used to play as kids."

One more strike against Susannah, if that's what happened. "Why don't you ask Pru where she heard it?"

"I already did, and she said she couldn't exactly remember."

"What about having a word with the Frosties? Maybe you could ask them not to spread it around any further."

"I can do that," Philippa said.

~ ~ ~

Lill called the next day. "Josephine, you better

come right away. It's Myrtle, and she's heard the rumor."

I didn't ask any questions, just grabbed my coat and keys and drove over to the main building. When I knocked on Lill's door, she opened it as if she'd been standing there waiting for me. But instead of motioning me inside, she stepped into the corridor and pulled the door almost shut behind her.

"Myrtle got this card in the mail today." She handed me an oversize greeting card. On the front were the words, "In Sympathy at the Loss of Your Loved One." *Loved One* was crossed out with black magic marker and replaced by *Son*. I opened the card to find it contained several short messages. The one supposedly from me said, "Nothing is more devastating than losing a child. I know exactly how that feels." Lill's message was, "I understand the pain of having a child who has strayed from the path of righteousness. I'm here for you. Your friend, Lillian."

"I know you didn't write that, and neither did I," Lill said. "I suspect one person did all of this, this hurtfulness."

Since Lill's a Graphoanalyst, she would know that, if anyone would.

"How's Myrtle doing?"

"Come see. I didn't tell her I was calling you, by the way. I didn't want her to leave."

I wasn't sure what Lill was suggesting. That my presence wouldn't be a comfort? Fair enough, I suppose. Susannah was mostly right about me being standoffish. Only recently have I begun to overcome that.

I followed Lill into her apartment. Myrtle was sitting at the table with a cup of tea and there was a plate of cookies in front of her, but she seemed to be ignoring both. That was all the proof I needed that she was not in a normal frame of mind.

"Myrtle," I said, slipping out of my coat and taking a seat across from her. "About this card."

She looked up from moving her spoon in circles on the tabletop. Her mascara had been washed away by tears, but luckily, she'd mostly managed to mop up the black streaks with several tissues that were now wadded together on the tabletop.

"Yes. Thank you, and Lillian, of course, for sending me such a thoughtful reminder of the worst day of my life." Her tone was flat, and she seemed flattened as well. I realized as she lifted her arm, she wasn't wearing her bracelets, so the cheerful jingle that usually accompanies her pronouncements was missing. That loss combined with her missing makeup made her appear pale and diminished, not at all the vibrant Myrtle I know.

"So whose idea was it to send me a card?"

Myrtle said, glaring first at Lill and then at me.

"Lill and I didn't sign this," I said, tapping the card.

"Then who?"

"We don't know, but we suspect it's the work of one person."

"Has everybody heard about this?"

I glanced at Lill, debating how to answer. With the truth, I decided. Painful as it might be.

"I'm afraid so. You see, a rumor started a couple of days ago. That your son murdered someone, actually."

"So you're saying everybody's heard about this? But you didn't tell me."

"We hoped it would just die out. And we did try to stop it."

She hitched in a breath and blew her nose.

"It isn't true, you know. He didn't murder anyone. He was killed in an accident. Why would someone say such an awful, awful thing?"

Lill placed a hand on Myrtle's arm. "We don't know. We're terribly sorry this is happening to you."

Myrtle continued to sit, sniffing and blotting her eyes. "So, you don't have any idea who started it?" she asked.

"We don't. We thought about trying to find

out when we first heard. But by that time, so many people knew about it from so many different sources, it was impossible to track down."

"Why would someone do this?" Myrtle said. "It's cruel." She'd stopped crying, but there was a catch in her voice.

"Have you ever told anyone about losing your son?" Lill asked, slipping effortlessly into investigator mode.

"No. Never. I try not to think about it if I can help it. You see, he was killed right before his wedding. It was so long ago, I can sometimes go months without thinking of that horrible time." She started to cry again.

"I'm sorry," I said. "That someone would try to hurt you this way." I paused to give her another moment to compose herself. "Do you have the envelope the card came in?"

Sniffing, she reached in her tote and pulled out an envelope and passed it to me. The address was neatly printed, but there was no return address even though it had been mailed. Usually when someone suffers a loss, a friend or the manager passes around a card for everyone to sign, and then it's placed directly in the person's mailbox.

"I think it has to be a new resident doing this," Myrtle said.

Precisely my thought. And I had the perfect

candidate in mind. Susannah. It was exactly the sort of sly, nasty thing I could see her doing. But why would she pick on Myrtle? They were supposed to be friends, weren't they?

"I'm thinking it might be that Glory person," Myrtle said. "I don't think she likes me. And I must say it's mutual after she stole that seat on the board from me. She knew I wanted it, and yet in she swooped, and that was that."

Clearly, she'd just transitioned from upset to full-on anger.

"Why don't you let Lill and me investigate? Lill can examine the writing to see if more than one person was involved, and I can do some checking." I wasn't entirely certain what I'd check—fingerprints on the card? DNA on the envelope adhesive, maybe?

"Is there anything else you'd like us to do?" Lill asked Myrtle after I'd gotten her permission to carry off the envelope.

"Oh, I'll be fine," she said, dabbing at a tear. "I learned a long time ago not to dwell on the tragedies of life."

Lill and I exchanged a glance. We knew how much Myrtle dwelt on what we'd always thought was her main tragedy—that she'd been sabotaged during a beauty pageant. But this time, she was totally ignoring a plate of cookies. Not a good sign.

Although Myrtle can be annoying at times, she doesn't deserve this kind of treatment. No one does.

Chapter Eight

Lillian

I paused in the doorway to the dining room, looking for Glory. Like Myrtle and Susannah, Glory and I have made a habit of eating together.

Some of the residents sitting at nearby tables stopped speaking and stared at me. Even people with their backs to the door turned to look before they turned back to whisper to their companions.

The glares felt eerily familiar, as did the whispers. I've encountered them off and on my entire life, in grocery stores and when I shopped at Lord & Taylors and occasionally at a Music Hall concert. That sense of people looking at me then dismissing me as a lesser being because my skin is darker than theirs. But it had never before happened here at Brookside. Oh, occasionally someone used an insensitive adjective, but usually that someone was a person who was beginning to slip mentally, so I gave them a pass.

I gave my head a sharp shake, convinced as

people resumed their conversations that I was imagining that the disgruntled looks, if that's what they were, were aimed at me.

I didn't see Glory, but then Edna had walked up behind me during that odd interval of staring. Now she did a quick scan of the room and took my arm. "Let's sit over there, shall we? We two pariahs together."

I didn't understand what she meant, but I let her lead the way to a two-person table.

"I should have called you," Edna said, as we sat down. "But I hoped it would all die down, like it did with Myrtle, and mostly has with me."

"What would die down?"

"The rumor about you."

"What rumor?"

"The one about your husband being a drug dealer. He got shot, but you managed to hold onto the money, and that's how you can afford to live here."

"What? Are you serious?"

"As a case of poison ivy. It's not true, is it?"

"Of course it's not true." I closed my eyes, thinking of my dear Roger, who had been a teacher like me, and the kindest man I've ever known. "Who told you?"

"The Frosties."

It was clear that Norman's nickname for the

pair was catching on.

"And when I asked them where they heard it, they just tittered and said everybody knew."

Which they clearly did, based on the nasty looks I'd just gotten from the entire room. I glanced around, noticing that a couple of sheets of paper were being passed from table to table, and that most people seemed to be glancing over at me before signing them.

"What do you think that's about?" I asked Edna.

"I'll just go and find out, shall I?" Edna got up and walked over to the nearest table where one of the papers had just landed. Without a word, she reached in, grabbed the paper, and returned to our table.

"Oh, my," she said, as she looked it over. Then she passed it to me. It was a petition, asking the Brookside manager to take immediate action to kick me out of Brookside since I was paying my fees with ill-gotten gains. It already had seven signatures, and since there were at least three sheets being passed around, it meant the idea of getting rid of me was gaining a good deal of support. I was still staring at the page when a hand reached over my shoulder and snatched it away.

"You can't just help yourself to other people's property." The man who'd grabbed the sheet was a newer resident. Someone I'd never spoken to, except perhaps to greet in the hallway. When I turned to look at him, he gave me such an angry glare, I froze in place.

Edna stood, and was clearly ready to arm wrestle the man for the paper, even though he was at least twenty years younger and not at all tottery. I put a hand on her arm to restrain her. "It's all right, Edna. Let the man have his paper."

"You've got that right," the man said.

He walked away, and I watched him rejoin his companions. They stared back at me with triumphant looks.

"I don't feel hungry," I said.

"You cannot give them the satisfaction of running you off. You have to stick around and at least pretend you're eating, Lillian. They're bullies. Every last one of them, and I'm taking names."

As a teacher, I've had a lot of experience with bullies, so I knew she was right about me needing to stand up for myself and not run away. But it wasn't easy getting through that meal. Mostly I moved food around my plate to make it look like I'd eaten something, but I felt too nauseated to put a bite in my mouth. Edna left me alone and ate her meal, but once our plates were cleared, she said we didn't have to stay for dessert.

"What I think we need to do now is call Josephine," she said.

"Yes, I suppose so." I'd transitioned from the adrenaline surge when I saw what was on the paper to a lassitude that made it hard for me to keep my eyes open.

Edna stood and waited for me to stand and then, head held high, she walked with me out of the room.

"Your place or mine?" she asked once we were out in the hall.

"Mine, I think."

When we arrived, Edna walked in and picked up my phone. "What's Josephine's number?"

I told her, and while she dialed, I sank onto the sofa, wishing I could simply lie down and sleep.

"Josephine, it's Edna. I'm here with Lillian, and you and Norman need to come right now. No, no, it's not a medical problem. We'll explain when you get here."

By the time she hung up, I'd given in and curled up on the couch and closed my eyes. But I couldn't seem to erase from my mind the angry looks I'd just received from both people who'd previously been friendly, along with ones who were mostly unknown to me. Had I fooled myself about being accepted at Brookside? It shouldn't be an issue, of course. After all, I don't think any White residents worry about being accepted.

There was a knock, and Edna went to open the door. Reluctantly, I sat up and rubbed at my eyes.

Josephine came immediately and sat next to me, taking one of my hands in hers. "What is it, Lill? What's going on?"

Since I was having trouble putting words together, Edna spoke. "There's another rumor, like the one about Myrtle, but this one's much worse."

"Well, what is it?"

"That Lillian's husband was a drug dealer, and that's how she can afford to live here," Edna said, speaking quickly and without emotion. "And someone has started circulating a petition to get Lillian kicked out of Brookside."

"Oh, Lill. That's, that's horrible," Josephine said, pulling me into a hug.

Josephine is not much of a spontaneous hugger, so I knew the story had upset her.

There was another knock on the door, and Norman, who was closest, went to answer it.

"Where is she? I need to see her immediately." The visitor was Myrtle. I gave Josephine a pleading look. I simply didn't know if I could deal with Myrtle right now. But being Myrtle, she simply shoved her walker forward, forcing Norman to step out of the way.

"Lillian, I just heard. I was out to dinner with my granddaughter, but I wasn't back two seconds before I had several people regaling me with some vile story about you and asking me to sign a scurrilous document. When I saw what that document was, I'll have you know I tore it into confetti. They sure didn't like it, I can tell you that. They may want to get rid of me next."

As she spoke, Myrtle made her way into the room and plopped into my one easy chair.

"Did you get a card?" Myrtle asked.

"A card?"

"You know, like I did when that cruel rumor about my son went round."

"No, no card."

"Well, I don't suppose Hallmark has something that would quite fit this situation. So what are we going to do about it?"

We?

Thankfully, she was interrupted by another knock. This time, it was Philippa and Richard. Since they rarely eat in the dining room, they'd just heard the news when someone showed up at their door asking them to sign the petition to remove me.

My apartment isn't very big, so the room was becoming quite crowded. Someone grabbed the chairs from my dinette table and everyone found a seat.

"This is just dreadful," Myrtle said. "What was done to me was cruel, but what's being done to

Lillian is criminal, and whoever's responsible for this is the one who should be kicked out. It makes me furious."

"You think it's the same person doing all this?" I asked.

"Don't you? I think it has to be someone who recently arrived. After all, think about what we've all been through. I mean, consider Edna. She did some pretty bad things. Sorry, Edna, it's true, and I just have to say it. But nobody organized a smear campaign or lobbied to get her kicked out."

"Well, there was that note about me posted on the bulletin board," Edna said.

Myrtle's face took on a determined look. She shook off Edna's comment. "I suspect that so-called Glorious Pennycutt," she said.

She'd suggested Glory as a suspect before. But she didn't know Glory the way I did.

"I'm quite sure she's not responsible. After all, what would be her motive?"

"Some people just like to stir things up and then sit back and watch."

"But she isn't watching. Besides, Glory's my friend. I think it's more likely to be—"

"Why don't we wait until we can investigate," Josephine said, cutting me off. I glanced at her, and she gave her head a little shake. And it hit me that she knew I was going to accuse Susannah, and that would have drawn the same response from Myrtle that her accusing Glory had gotten from me.

"We need to alert the manager to what's happening before these petitions land on her desk," Norman said.

"You're right," Josephine said, pulling out her phone and moving toward the door. "I'll call Marge." Marge is the manager.

"You need to tell us about your husband," Myrtle said. "Is there even a shred of truth in what's being said?"

"Roger and I both taught school in Cincinnati. The only drugs involved were the ones Roger confiscated from the older students. And as for the money to pay for Brookside, we watched our pennies our whole lives so we would have a nice retirement." I didn't feel I had to tell them that the other reasons I could afford Brookside were the stock options I'd gotten while consulting as a Graphoanalyst and the life insurance I received after Roger's heart attack.

"Well, I didn't believe a word of it was true," Myrtle said. "But even if it were true, I'd still be your friend, Lillian."

Myrtle may frequently annoy me, but she'd just proven herself to be a true friend, standing by my side when so many people had stepped away. And I wasn't surprised that the others who crowded my living room had shown up immediately to support me. Not one of them was a fake friend.

But what about Glory? I hadn't seen her at dinner, and usually she let me know if she wasn't going to be there. So her absence was difficult to explain. I wondered if, after hearing the rumor, she'd decided to avoid me. I think young people call that ghosting. I didn't want to believe it. In fact, I wouldn't. Not until I spoke to her.

"I just talked to Marge," Josephine said, walking back in. "She's very disturbed by what's happening. She's going to call a meeting of the board in the morning."

Josephine came back to take the seat beside me. I leaned over and whispered in her ear, asking if she could get everyone to leave. I was feeling overwhelmed by both the anger that had been directed at me in the dining room and the support they were all now providing.

"I think that's all we can do right now," Josephine said. "And we need to let Lill have some quiet time."

Philippa immediately stood and pulled Richard to his feet. "Of course. Myrtle, Edna, why don't we walk you back to your apartments?"

"Yes," Myrtle said, heaving herself to her feet. "I suppose you're right, Josephine. But you have my number, Lillian. Don't you hesitate for one instant to call me if you need company."

I thanked her, but breathed a sigh of relief when the four of them left.

Josephine turned off the bright overhead lights. "Do you want me to make you a cup of tea, Lill?"

"No. Yes. I mean, that would be nice."

"Let me," Norman said, leaving the two of us.

"I appreciate that everyone came, but I'm so glad they're gone now," I told Josephine.

"It was a bit overwhelming," she agreed. "Do you want to talk about it?"

"It was the shock, you know. I really thought . . ."

"I know. You thought you'd found a place free of prejudice. But Lill, you know there are bigots and racists everywhere."

"But nobody here has ever treated me that way before."

"Are you sure?"

I thought about that as Norman handed me a mug of tea.

"Well, of course, there have been occasional incidents." I spoke reluctantly, still not wanting to believe that any snubs had been due to more than poor eyesight. I also didn't want to believe the ones who began muttering to themselves as they walked past me could possibly have been cursing me under their breath. But now . . .

I held the mug, letting it warm my hands, knowing I didn't want to live differently. I didn't want to always be on the lookout for hidden agendas and racism. But would I be able to avoid looking for it, suspecting it, after what had just happened?

Although, to be fair, some of the looks may have merely been ones of avid curiosity rather than hostility. For many residents, anything that offers a little drama is welcome since most of our days are so uneventful.

"Would you like to stay with us for a while?" Josephine asked, and I realized I was still holding the tea but hadn't taken a sip.

"I think I'll be all right. It really helped that everyone came. Except." *Glory.*

"What is it?" Josephine asked.

"Oh, nothing. I'll be fine." I set the mug down. "I'm exhausted. If you don't mind, I think I'll go to bed."

"I want you to come for breakfast," Josephine said. "Why don't you give us a call when you're ready, and one of us will pick you up."

"Yes, I'd like that."

Josephine, excellent friend that she is, picked up the mugs of tea and carried them to the kitchen. She came back and kissed me on the cheek. Another thing Josephine doesn't usually do. And then she and Norman let themselves out.

Chapter Nine

Josephine

I cannot remember the last time I've been this angry. By the time Norman and I walked back to our car for the short drive to our house, I was shaking with it. I'd managed to hold it in while we were with Lill, because I could tell anger wouldn't help the situation, or her.

It wasn't just the rumor that disturbed me. It was the speed with which it had been accepted and acted upon. It stunned me that people who had known Lill for years could apparently harbor so much ill will that they would take immediate steps to have her tossed out on the basis of a rumor. It was as if they were just waiting for something like this to express their dislike.

"What are we going to do about this?" I asked.

Norman waited until we were in the house to answer me.

"To start with, I'll be at that board meeting tomorrow morning. I've already gotten a text from Marge about it."

"Oh. When did that happen?"

"About five minutes after you spoke to her."

"Those meetings are open to everyone, aren't they?"

"Usually. But she's asked that we meet in executive session, so only board members can attend."

I might not like it, but at least Norman would be there. Besides, I needed to be available for Lill's call. Until this was sorted out, I intended to make sure she ate with us, especially after Edna made a quick detour on the way out to whisper in my ear that Lill hadn't eaten a bite of her dinner.

~ ~ ~

The next morning, Norman left for the board meeting, and shortly after that, Lill called. I picked her up, brought her back, and cooked us omelets. After what Edna said about dinner, I was relieved when she cleaned her plate. Lill has always had a good appetite, even though she stays as skinny as a fence post. I told her Norman was at the board meeting.

"I'm trying to decide if that'll make a

difference, folk being what they are."

"These particular *folk* are sheep, and whoever's the source of this is an adept psychologist who knew the exact button to push. He, or she, knew that when those old biddies heard the words *drug dealer*, they'd act before they took even a moment to stop and think about it. But you need to know you have plenty of true friends who will stand by you, starting with me."

"I do know that." She sighed. "I really thought I was done with dirty and dismissive looks and people whispering about me behind my back."

"I know. I hate that this is happening to you."

"You suspect Susannah, don't you? But you didn't want me to accuse her last night."

"I didn't want you saying her name in front of Myrtle. She thinks Susannah's her friend, and I'm sure she'd say something to her."

"But I barely know Susannah. Why would she want to hurt me?"

"Possibly because you're my friend."

"So, it's you she's trying to hurt?"

"I think it's possible."

"But why? What does she gain?"

"I'm not saying I'm right or that I understand what motive she might have. But you do remember that look she gave me at the Christmas party."

"That look was downright evil. Like the looks I got last night." She shuddered. "So are you thinking maybe Philippa or Richard will be her next target? And if so, what do we do about it?"

"We begin by first putting a stop to the rumor about you. And we make sure we warn Philippa and Richard, although I'm guessing they may already be bracing for it."

We'd finished our omelets and were taking our time with our tea when Norman returned from the board meeting. He sat at the table with us and poured himself a cup of coffee.

"So?" I said. "What happened?"

"Everyone was there, except Glory. The manager said she'd texted that she was with a friend at the hospital and would be unable to attend."

"Oh," Lill said. "I'm glad to know she's okay. I was worried about her."

"And you wondered why she didn't show up last night," I said.

"Yes. I thought it was odd, or that maybe she'd heard and believed the rumor."

"Glory doesn't strike me as a person who'd jump to conclusions without checking the evidence," Norman said.

"So, what happened at the meeting?" I asked.

"Everyone on the board had heard the rumor,

although when they all thought back to who told them, there was no common thread. Marge found the petition slipped under her door when she arrived this morning. There were twenty signatures in all, although some of them were indecipherable. All the board members said they'd either not been asked to sign or had refused."

"Twenty is only a small fraction of the residents," I said. "And it sounds like signatures could have been forged."

"I saw people signing," Lill said. "Some may be forged or made up, but there were definitely people who agreed with the petitioner, whoever that is."

"Nobody knew who that might be, though, right?" I asked Norman.

He shook his head. "Although, it appears that one Andrew Winston has been happy to help things along."

"Did you reach any sort of consensus on what to do?" I asked.

"Well, first, I told everyone what I know about you, Lill, and that the rumor has no basis in fact. I said that if any of them had any doubts at all, I'd be happy to speak further with them. But my take is that everyone was appalled at what was going on, and nobody questioned that the rumor was anything but false."

"What about the people who think it's true?

The ones who signed?"

"Marge is going to speak privately with everyone whose signature she can make out. Then it's her intention to have a general meeting to discuss the corrosive effect gossiping about fellow residents can have. She's also going to say that anybody who initiates such rumors might be liable to eviction."

"Would they be?"

"Unlikely. But the bylaws do allow for it. And knowing that might be enough to stop whoever is doing this. Although, I must say, whoever it is has so far managed to cover their tracks pretty well. The consensus was that it was most likely a newer resident."

"Because why would the people who've known Myrtle and Edna and Lill for years suddenly start doing something like this. Is that what you're thinking?" I said.

"Pretty much."

"Well, I think it's Susannah," I said. "She's the only person I know who's nasty enough to do something like this."

"You can't just accuse her, Jo," Norman said.

"I know. We're going to need evidence. For starters, I need the names of the people who signed the petition."

"Now, Jo, why don't we let Marge do her

thing before we jump in? If it is Susannah doing this, knowing she's upset you will be exactly what she's going for."

"Do not, *now Jo* me, Norman Neuman. You did have Marge make a copy of the petition, didn't you?"

Norman sighed, but I know my man. He pulled the pages from his pocket and handed them to me. Lill and I bent over them. I grabbed a pencil and we wrote down the names we could decipher.

We ended with a list of ten people that included one of the Frosties, Bertie, Pru Parker, and Andrew Winston.

"Well, we know for sure it had to be a woman egging Pru on, since none of the men will go near her," I said, looking at the list. I could only vaguely picture some of the signers, but after all, I moved out of my apartment in the main building some time ago, and besides, no one would ever accuse me of being a social butterfly.

"It's interesting that only one of the Frosties signed this, and yet they're always together. So it might be worthwhile asking them about it."

Norman sighed. "There's nothing I can say that's going to stop you, is there."

"Shouldn't have given me a copy."

"Try to be diplomatic, then."

"When have I ever not been diplomatic?"

Norman just shook his head at me and winked at Lill, who chuckled. That chuckle gave me hope that Lill wasn't going to suffer any permanent damage from this. I was still worried about her, though.

"I want to go with you to talk to people," Lill said.

I was going to say I didn't think it was a good idea, but then I decided that since the malice was aimed at her, she had a right to confront these people. Besides, if I said no, she could just go on her own, and I was absolutely certain that was not a good idea, so I nodded and said we'd do it together.

"Starting with Pru," Lill said.

"Okay."

"Now?" Lill said.

"Don't you think it would be wise to give Marge a chance to talk to everyone first?" Norman said.

"I really need to get started on this," Lill said.

"Okay. Let's go talk to Pru." Personally, I thought Pru would be one of the least helpful people to talk to. But perhaps that was the point. Pick off the weakest links first.

Norman shooed us out the door, saying he'd take care of the dishes. That was sweet of him. I'm a disorganized cook, so I usually leave the kitchen in major disarray even when all I'm cooking is something simple, like an egg.

I grabbed a coat and keys and drove with Lill back to the main building.

"Do you know which apartment Pru is in?" I asked when we arrived at the back door.

"She's in Lark-Tulip."

The various wings of the main building have all been christened with combination bird and plant names that residents shorten for convenience. Pru's wing's full name is the Meadow Lark-Tulip wing.

Lill led the way, and when we reached the first apartment in that wing, she stopped.

"Okay, Josephine. Let's see how good a detective you are."

I looked at the closest doors, seeing Christmas wreaths on three out of the four of them. Two entrances also had small tables by the doors. One held a red poinsettia; another had a large bowl filled with candies. The third door had a large ceramic sheepdog sitting off to the side wearing a Santa hat with a red and green scarf knotted around its neck.

"What's with the dog?" I asked Lill.

"Oh, that's Fernando. Or a reasonable facsimile," Lill said.

"It's ugly."

"But you have to admit he's stylish, not to

mention seasonally appropriate. You really need to check him out next Halloween."

I shook my head at the thought. When I lived in the Glory-Dove wing, I'd resisted the custom of decorating my door. But here in Lark-Tulip I could see the tradition was going strong, except for one door. It carried a placard that declared: Women Rule the World. Well, it had started out as Men Rule the World, but someone had added the necessary two letters to "men" to change the message. And those letters were written in wobbly black marker, reminding me of Myrtle's pseudo sympathy card.

"Too easy," I said, glancing at Lill.

She shrugged. "No one can accuse Pru of being repressed."

"No they cannot."

I pushed the doorbell. After a couple of minutes, we heard a shuffle approaching the door, and a moment later, it opened a crack, and we could see Pru peering at us.

"You don't have that penis with you, do you?"

I assumed Pru was addressing me and referring to Norman. I told her it was only a couple of vaginas calling on her. She snorted and pulled the door open and waved us in.

"What do you want?" she said, leading us to

seats in her tiny living area.

I pulled out the sheet of paper with her signature and handed it to her. "We want to know about this. Who asked you to sign it and why did you do so?"

She peered at the paper, then asked me to hand her the reading glasses on an end table near where I was sitting. I did so and then sat back down. With Lill, I watched her mouthing the words as she read through the paper.

She looked up, frowning. "Well, yes. It does look like I signed it, but this ain't what I thought I was signing."

"What did you think it was?"

"Darlene was the one brung it over during dinner. Said it was a request they serve chocolate pudding more often. I do like chocolate pudding, you know." She glanced at us, her eyes magnified behind the lenses of her glasses. "Took her word that's what it was about. So your man was a drug dealer?"

"No. He wasn't."

"Wouldn't surprise me none if he were," Pru said, seemingly ignoring Lill's response. "Men are the most useless of all God's creatures. Get rid of 'em, we won't have to worry about climate change. You know what I'm saying?"

I didn't dare exchange a glance with Lill, as I was too close to the edge of hilarity to risk it.

"Am I to understand you wouldn't have

signed the paper if you'd known what it was about?" I asked.

"Course not. Trying to evict someone 'cause of something some man did. Ain't right. 'Sides, I ain't got nothing against Lillian. Youse are good people. Don't like being lied to, neither. Think I'll give that Darlene a piece of my mind."

"Oh, I wouldn't do that," I said. "I suspect someone told Darlene the same story she told you."

"Likely you're right. I swear that Darlene don't have two brain cells to rub together. Not like you two."

I signaled Lill, and we both stood and took our leave of Pru.

"You certainly have a unique door decoration," I said as we opened the door.

"My granddaughter mostly done it for me. I'll tell her you liked it." It wasn't exactly what I'd said. But close enough. And Pru had a granddaughter? That was a surprise.

"That Andrew Winston don't like it, let me tell you. Even complained to the manager. She said there weren't nothing in the bylaws against it. Tickled me no end."

"Good for you," I said, remembering what Edna and Lill had shared about their interaction with Andrew Winston at dinner.

As the uniquely decorated door closed behind us, I asked Lill if she knew where Darlene lived.

"I do. In Snap-Tit, right next door to Myrtle." Snap-Tit is shorthand for Snapdragon-Titmouse, and whoever picked it was either oblivious or had a wicked sense of humor.

We rang Darlene's doorbell and were once again successful. She looked a bit uncomfortable when she opened the door and found Lill standing next to me.

"Oh, it's you," she said, glancing at Lill and then back at me. "I'm getting ready to go out, an important medical appointment, so I really don't have time to talk to you right now."

I didn't believe her, given she was wearing a housecoat and bunny slippers.

"This will take only a moment," I said, moving into the doorway so she couldn't close the door on me. "We have a simple question for you. Why did you tell Pru Parker the petition you were asking her to sign was a request that the kitchen serve chocolate pudding more often?"

She started blinking rapidly. "Well, we needed signatures, didn't we? I mean, don't you just do that? Tell people what they want to hear?"

"Who started the petition?"

"I don't know, do I? I mean it arrived at our table when we weren't looking, and once we saw what it was about we all decided to sign, and then Andrew suggested I get Pru Parker to sign, and I had to tell her something."

"You're saying Pru signed to get more pudding. Why did you sign?"

"Well, we can't have drug dealers here, can we?"

"Lill isn't a drug dealer."

"But she was married to one. Same difference."

"She wasn't," I said.

"How do we know? I mean, she could've been."

"She's right here. Why don't you ask her?"

Darlene looked everywhere but at Lill while the two of us stood in her doorway, waiting.

"Oh, okay. Was your husband a drug dealer and are you living off his ill-gotten gains? Although, I don't know why you would expect me to believe anything you say."

"And why is that?" I asked, fighting the impulse to grab Darlene by the big bow at the neck of her flowery housecoat and give it a yank. What an irritating woman.

"Well, she's one of those people, isn't she?"

"What people?" I asked.

She waved a hand. "You know. *Those* people."

"You mean Black people?" I said.

"You know exactly what I'm saying."

"I'm hoping I don't," I said. "But here's what I'm thinking, and you'll have to tell me if I'm wrong." Something had snapped inside me, freeing me from my usual careful speech. "You're thinking you're better than my friend here because you have crepey beige skin with ugly brown spots, while hers is a nice shade of brown all over."

Somewhere in the middle of my rant, Lill had laid a hand on my arm and begun pulling. "Not worth it, Josephine," she said, for at least the second time.

"Well I never," Darlene sputtered. "I'm done talking to you. And her. I want you to leave immediately. If you don't I'm pulling my emergency cord."

"We're happy to leave. It's really most unpleasant being in the presence of a person with such limited cognitive ability."

Lill jerked, I stepped back, and Darlene slammed the door.

"Well, I guess we know what she thinks about things," I said to Lill as I stood straightening my blouse. Taking that last shot at Darlene had felt good, but now the reality of her attitude toward Lill, one of my favorite people, took over and made me feel a bit sick, not to mention annoyed with myself.

"I'm sorry, Lill. I shouldn't have done that, should I?"

"Probably not."

"It felt good, though."

"Won't make any difference. That woman's too old and set in her ways to change her thinking now."

"I know. I don't know what got into me."

"A little righteous indignation. And I appreciate it. You know I do. But I don't think it does much good."

"I suppose if it did, things would be a lot different by now."

"I need a break," Lill said. "Think I'll go check in with Glory, and then I'm going to take a nap."

"Okay. I'll pick you up for lunch, at noon?"

She shook her head. "I need to get back to my routine. If Glory's not available, I'll call Edna or Myrtle and go to lunch with them."

We parted at her apartment door, and I let her think I was leaving. Instead, as soon as I rounded the corner, I pulled out my phone and called reception to ask which apartment the Frosties were in, and then I made my way there.

Midmorning is clearly an excellent time for visiting, since their door also opened promptly. They both stuck their heads into the gap and, seeing me, twittered with excitement. The door opened wider, and they ushered me into a living room that was decorated within an inch of its life with red and green wreaths, baubles, and bows.

"My goodness, Josephine, whatever brings you to our humble abode? You do know this is a major honor. We're so excited to see you, aren't we, Martha? Come, come, you must sit. Would you like some eggnog?"

"Of course she does. I'll go get it, shall I?"

"Turn down the music while you're at it."

"Please, no. No eggnog. I just ate breakfast, and I'm still quite full."

"Oh. Well, that is a disappointment. Martha's eggnog is famous, you know."

"Perhaps another time."

Martha perched on the edge of a chair and leaned toward me. "Well, if you're not here for eggnog, might I be so bold as to ask the purpose of your visit?"

"I'm following up on a mystery." I was determined to be more diplomatic this time. And also determined to keep the two women straight. Martha was more serious, Mary, more the flitterer.

"Oh, we just love mysteries, don't we, Martha."

"Indeed we do. Almost as much as we love eggnog," Martha said, her tone a bit sniffy.

Since Mary was the one who'd signed the petition, I turned toward her.

"I have a question for you, Mary. Well, really for the two of you. But mostly for Mary. Last night at dinner, a petition was passed around. You signed it, but Martha didn't, and I was wondering if you could tell me why?"

Mary sat back, beginning to wring her hands.

"You didn't sign it, did you?" Martha asked.

"Oh, dear, I'm afraid so," Mary said, her head shaking. "I knew I shouldn't, but Andrew insisted."

"Andrew Winston?" I said.

"Yes."

"Did you read it to see what it was about?"

"He said it was about getting rid of a person who was a known drug dealer."

"Did he say who the person was?"

"Well, he sort of did."

"How sort of?"

"He said it was Lillian Fitzel." By this time, Mary was bent over, rocking and giving me quick glances as I continued to question her.

"Did he say who told him Lill was a drug dealer?"

"He just said everybody knew it, and it was time somebody did something about it. And I said maybe we should make sure it was true, and he said he had it on very good authority it was true, and that if I didn't sign, I was letting down all my fellow residents."

I sat back, trying to fit what Mary was saying into the puzzle of who started the whole thing. Meanwhile, Martha got up from her chair and went over to Mary.

"I thought we agreed we didn't know enough to sign it."

"But then you went to talk to Evelyn, and you left me there with Andrew, and you know how insistent he can be."

"But we'd decided that we needed to speak with Lillian first."

"You decided." Mary's voice had gone up in pitch, and she'd stopped rocking.

I sat back, watching the dynamic develop.

"It wasn't something to be done on the spur of the moment," Martha insisted.

"Like that thing with the Culpeppers, you mean?" Mary said. "And anyway, Andrew wasn't doing it on the spur of the moment. He'd done his research, and he said it was true. We can't always sit on the sidelines waiting for who knows what to come along."

"You were the one who decided to turn Ronald down, and you did it completely on your own," Martha said.

"I never would have done it if it hadn't been for you."

Clearly, they were no longer talking about the petition.

"I could have had a family," Mary said. "But no. Ronald wasn't good enough, was he? Says you. I needed to wait until someone better came along. Except nobody ever did. Did they? And now look where we are."

"We're here, aren't we? In a very nice place where—"

"I hope you don't think I'm being rude, but I have an appointment, you see." As I spoke, I'd stood and backed in the direction of the front door.

"It was so nice of you to visit," Martha said, without missing a beat. "Let me show you out."

Relieved, I turned and made my escape. As I walked away, I debated whether to go speak to Andrew Winston now or leave it for later when maybe Lill could come with me. But then, on second thought, I wasn't at all certain it would be a good idea to confront the man with Lill in tow after the way he'd treated her last night.

No, better to just go myself and get it over with. And I wasn't going to think about what Norman would say about that. But since it sounded like Andrew had assumed a major role in getting signatures for the petition, that meant he might also know more about who the instigator was.

Once again, I called the front desk and asked for an apartment number. The girl manning the desk said, "My goodness you're having quite a busy morning."

"It does seem so."

"Well Andrew's in Snap-Tit. Number fourteen." Staff are not supposed to use the nicknames, especially that one.

I hesitated when I got to his door. There was a bare evergreen wreath hanging there, needles beginning to dry out and drop, but the entrance was otherwise lacking in decorative touches. I barely knew Andrew, and I couldn't even say for sure whether he was married, but that question was immediately dealt with when a pale woman answered the door. She peered at me with a look that suggested she expected to find a mugger on her doorstep.

She cocked her head. "Yes?"

"Mrs. Winston?"

"Yes. And you are?"

"I'm Josephine Neuman. I'd like to speak to your husband. Is he here?"

"Oh, no. Andrew's at the gym. He always goes from nine fifteen to ten twenty. Every day."

I glanced at my watch. It was now ten fifteen. It meant I faced a choice. Walk over to the gym and wait for Andrew to exit or engage his wife in conversation until he returned. I decided engagement was worth a shot, despite the woman's tentative demeanor.

"Could I maybe come in and wait for him?"

"Oh, I don't think he'd like that. Andrew is very particular about who he invites in."

"What about you? Don't you get a say?"

"I don't need a say. Everything Andrew does is for my good. He takes such wonderful care of me, you know. So I don't like to cause him any upset."

Her bland personality was matched by her appearance. She wore light gray sweats that appeared to be at least two sizes too large, and her eyes were a pale blue that might have been startling on someone with healthy skin tones and hair that wasn't colorless. Altogether, she looked like a woman who was trying to blend into the wallpaper. And mostly succeeding. Plus, she spoke so softly, I needed to lean in to hear it all.

"You don't go to the gym with him?" I said.

"Of course not. Andrew needs his space. If I was there, I'd distract him. He's very focused during his workouts."

I wondered briefly how Andrew dealt with the lack of space in a one-bedroom apartment.

"I go after he gets back," she added, explaining the sweats. "We have a routine, you see."

"You didn't tell me your name," I said.

"Chantelle."

That had me blinking. I was expecting something prosaic and, dare I say, dull, not something poetic.

"That's a lovely name." I hoped that didn't sound patronizing.

"Yes. I quite like it."

I glanced at my watch again. Ten seventeen. Waiting for Andrew required only the simple matter of filling a few more minutes with inane small talk.

"Have you been at Brookside long? I don't believe I've seen you before."

"We came in September. So not long."

"How do you like it?"

"Mostly we do. But we didn't expect we'd have to deal with any minorities actually living here. That's something they forgot to mention when we visited."

"Minorities?"

"Well, of course, we expected there to be staff members of the minority persuasion. Just not any as fellow residents."

Minority persuasion?

"And then, come to find out, that woman has connections to a drug dealer and his filthy lucre."

Filthy lucre? Who used that term anymore? By this time, my jaw was clenched and my fingernails were digging into my palms. I struggled to take in a calming breath, but it did little to calm me.

"So, how did you hear about the supposed connection of this minority persuasion resident to a drug dealer?"

"Not supposed at all!" Her volume increased, and I took a step back. "Several people told us about it, and they said when they asked the manager to do something, the manager refused."

"Which people?"

"Well, that old guy. Fred something? And, and Darlene."

Darn. Still no connection to Susannah. I was so concentrated on what Chantelle was saying that I missed seeing Andrew approach.

"Who's this, then, Ellie?" he said, making me jump.

"Oh, Andrew, this is . . . what did you say your name was?"

"Josephine."

"Yes, right. Josephine." Chantelle's words were quick and breathless. "We were just talking about that Black woman who's living here on illegal drug money."

"Did you want to sign the petition?" Andrew said. "I'm still collecting signatures. The more we get, the better." He dropped his gym bag, and I moved my foot out from under it.

"I'll take care of this. You better get going,

Ellie, if you want to stay on schedule."

"Of course, Andrew. I just have to grab my bag." She disappeared from the doorway, and a moment later returned and stepped out. "Did you have a good workout, honey?"

"Yes. Yes. Now go on. I'll get Josephine's signature."

"Nice talking to you, hmm, Josephine." Chantelle—Ellie—slipped between us and scurried down the hall, turning at the corner to wave. Andrew ignored her.

"I'm curious about the petition," I said. "I'm wondering whose idea it was."

"Mine, of course."

"Why, of course?"

"I've been watching that woman walk around here like she owns the place. Makes my blood boil."

"Why?"

He blinked and looked at me more closely. His eyes narrowed. "You know, I believe I've seen you talking to her. Yes, I have. You're not here to sign the petition, are you?"

"Of course not. And you might want to give that whole idea some more thought."

"Why would I do that?"

"Fomenting unrest this way and spreading lies about someone. It's unpleasant, and it's illegal. And it might just be you who's asked to leave."

He reared back slightly. "It's not illegal to tell the truth."

"But this isn't the truth, you see. So, if you don't stop, now that you know it's a lie, that would make it illegal. Defamation, actually."

"Why would I take your word for this?"

"You can look up defamation for yourself. But as to what you're saying about Lill, I know her. So let me make this crystal clear for you. Lillian Fitzel was not married to a drug dealer. Her husband was a schoolteacher. And she's not paying her Brookside fees with drug money, but rather with the savings she and her husband accumulated for over fifty years. And you passing around this rumor, and not just passing it around, but taking aggressive action on the basis of what is a clear lie. If you do that now that you know better, well, that might even be considered a hate crime."

"You don't know what you're talking about, woman."

"I do, actually. But if you doubt me, I can arrange for you to chat with my very good friend Darren McElroy. In case you don't recognize the name, he's the chief of police, and he has a very dim view of anyone hurting Lill."

"Because he's one of them?"

Having already encountered this sort of

euphemism, I knew immediately what he meant. "Mac isn't African American, if that's what you're insinuating."

"I think you're lying, and I'd like you to leave."

"I'm not lying, but I'm happy to leave. It gives me hives to have to spend time in the company of someone as bigoted and unpleasant as you."

"Why, you bi—"

"Now, now, Mr. Winston. You need to watch your language, and getting that irate can't possibly be good for your blood pressure."

His face turned red. I backed up, putting more space between us and then I turned and walked away at a steady pace, suppressing the urge to break into a run. The heat of his glare followed me down the hall. As I turned the corner, I heard the *thunk* of the door being closed, and for a moment, I felt boneless. Being in the presence of someone so hateful had also made my stomach clench with nausea. What an awful, awful man. And his wife with the pretty name was just as ugly as he was.

I knew the minute I went home, Norman would know I was upset, and once I told him what I'd done, he'd serve up a dose of, "You shouldn't have talked to that man on your own, Jo."

I have to admit he'd be right. I did let myself get carried away in my effort to help Lill. Thank goodness she wasn't with me when I called on the Winstons.

I was so upset, as a matter of fact, I almost forgot I'd driven over to the main building. But as I neared the front door, I saw Myrtle sitting there, ready to accost anyone going in or out, and remembered we'd come in the back door and that's where my car was. I turned quickly and hurried away, sighing with relief when there was no cheery "Tu la ru," chasing me down the hall.

I got in the car, trying to decide what to do next. I wasn't yet ready to face Norman or to talk to Mac, but there was someone else I could talk to.

I called Devi and breathed a sigh of relief when she said she was free for lunch.

Chapter Ten

Devi

Josephine picked me up at the museum's staff entrance, and we drove the short distance to a Mount Adams cafe overlooking downtown Cincinnati that we both liked.

"What's up?" I asked after we'd placed our orders, because it was obvious something was. Josephine always calls me at least a week ahead to make a lunch date, usually in conjunction with one of her regular visits to her Edward Hopper painting.

My question opened the floodgates. She reminded me of what she'd told me about Susannah Rasmussen at the Christmas party, then went on to tell me about the rumors that had recently circulated at Brookside, the hurtful ones about Edna and Myrtle and now another, more sinister, one about Lillian.

"It's one thing to publicize true if unpleasant information about Edna or to attach a false story to the death of Myrtle's son. It's something else to activate bigotry and aim it at Lill."

I also heard full accounts of Josephine's investigations this morning and her interactions with some of the people who'd signed the petition to kick Lillian out of Brookside.

"So, you wanted my advice?" I said when all that information had been delivered.

"I'm not sure what to do next. Most people can't remember where they first heard either of the rumors, and no one saw the notice about Edna being posted. But I think Susannah's the one pulling all the strings. I don't know how to prove that, and if I accuse her directly, she'll simply deny it and then celebrate outwitting me."

"So?"

"I thought you might have some ideas."

"You could start a nasty rumor about Susannah."

"Yes. Yes, I could." She stopped and shook her head. "No, I'm pretty sure Norman and Lill wouldn't approve of that. Nor would Mac."

"Probably not. That wasn't serious. Sorry, but I don't have any other ideas. Do you mind if I tell Maddie? And I'll talk to Mac, of course."

"Please do. We can use all the help we can get."

"Okay, we'll see what we can come up with. You know, I'm glad you called because I wanted to talk to you about something, as well."

"What's that?"

"Lisa."

"Uh-oh."

"Uh-oh, indeed. Since Hiroko went back to Japan, she's shown up twice during the day, while we're at work. She says she wants to spend time with the twins, but then she says she has a doctor's appointment and takes off for an hour or two, leaving Mika with Annie."

"It seems Lisa has given us yet another definition of *chutzpah*," Josephine said. "What are you going to do about it?"

"Mac's going to talk to her, and I've told

Annie not to answer the door. It's hard, though. Mika is a darling, but Lisa drives us to distraction. And trying to stop her from taking advantage of us, or of Annie, makes us feel like Grinches."

"'Tis the season," Josephine said with a sigh.

~ ~ ~

When I arrived home that evening, primed to talk to Mac about what was happening at Brookside, he was clearly worried about something. Since lately any change in his mood was usually linked to something to do with Lisa, I waited until we'd put the twins to bed to ask him what was going on.

"Sorry, love. I hoped you wouldn't notice."

I gave him a steady look.

He sighed. "Our internet checker came across some odd posts today."

"You have an internet checker?" There's so much about his job Mac can't talk about that I've learned not to ask many questions.

"Not officially, just a couple of the guys who are tech savvy, keeping an eye on things. We find it helps to keep track of what people from the area are posting. Sometimes we get a tip about someone stealing from mailboxes or breaking into cars before the victims get around to letting us know."

"But today was something different?"

"Here, I better show you." Mac went over to the laptop and, after a couple of minutes, stepped aside so I could see the site he'd loaded.

Montgomery Police Chief's Luxury Digs was the headline, followed by a picture of this house with a patrol car parked in front of it. Below that was the following:

> Recently named chief of police, Darren McElroy, his wife, and two young children live in this house off Hopewell Road in Montgomery. A check of property values indicates the house and the five acres it sits on are valued at nearly two million dollars. It seems curious that a small-town police chief can afford such a property, at least legitimately. Is our police chief perhaps moonlighting?

The poster had picked the screen name Shining-the-Light, and the site was one of the local sites that people use to post notices of lost dogs or requests for handyman references.

The original post was followed by a number of comments. I caught only a glimpse of the first one—someone thanking the poster for bringing such an obvious example of corruption to the attention of the residents of Montgomery—

because Mac pulled me away from the computer. I fought off a queasy feeling.

"What's being done about it?" I asked, swallowing.

"The city's lawyer is contacting the site to get it removed."

"But a lot of people have already seen it. There were several comments. Don't we need to issue a statement correcting the record?"

"We'll decide that later."

"Who decides? You and me?"

"No. Well, partly. But the city manager has been informed. So it'll probably be a joint decision. Although, anyone who takes the time to check would see we aren't the owners."

"But that might not satisfy them. They could still think there's something suspicious about us living here." I've found a lot of people are more than ready to take a leap to believing the worst of others. "Clearly, someone is trying to make you, or us, uncomfortable. So, is there anyone who has it in for you? Besides Lisa?"

She's never gotten over her snit from when Mac insisted she move into the apartment.

"I doubt it's Lisa," Mac said. "She might be tempted to post something nasty about me, but she wouldn't make something up or slant the truth this way. Besides, I don't think she's computer savvy enough to know how to do this and get away with it."

"So, maybe it's someone you've demoted? Fired? Arrested? Gave a ticket?" As I went through the list, Mac shook his head at each suggestion.

I took a deep breath. "This isn't the only news like this I've had today. Josephine took me to lunch so she could tell me what's going on at Brookside, and it's something similar."

I told Mac about the rumors and the subsequent petition to kick Lillian out of Brookside. "Isn't it illegal to do this sort of thing?"

"It is. It's called defamation," Mac said. "But it doesn't apply to the information about Edna, since that was true, or to the rumor about Myrtle, since it didn't harm her reputation or make people think ill of her. But the attack on Lill is another matter entirely."

"And on us."

"Yes. It appears both of those involve malice and fake information. That means the person or persons doing it could be charged either civilly or criminally."

"Do you think it's possible it's the same person?" I asked, thinking about what Josephine had said about Susannah.

"It's possible, I suppose. But it seems unlikely."

"Josephine has some potential physical evidence, but it only relates to the rumor about Myrtle."

"What is it?"

"The envelope the fake sympathy card came in had to be licked to seal it. Josephine's thinking about having it tested for DNA."

"What good is that?"

"She's planning to see if it matches a sample from the person she suspects. But she needs your help to know where to get the envelope tested."

"Who does she suspect?"

"Susannah Rasmussen."

"We're not going to be able to stop Jo investigating, are we."

"I'm not sure we want to."

Mac rolled his eyes and pulled out his phone. "I'll text her the name of a lab she can use. But why does she think Susannah's doing this?"

"To hurt her, by hurting her friends."

"And what exactly is Susannah's beef with Jo?"

"She tried to blackmail her."

"Oh, yeah. I remember now. And at the Christmas party you found her rifling the desk."

"Josephine did."

"Embarrassed her, I imagine. Clearly she has a motive, then."

I wasn't sure he was being completely serious, but I had managed to take his mind off the internet attack. At least for the moment.

Chapter Eleven

Lillian

Because I'd promised Josephine I would, I called Edna to make a date for lunch. I picked Edna because Glory was still with her friend who'd been moved to hospice, and I didn't want to call Myrtle because she usually eats with Susannah. Given Josephine's suspicions about Susannah—suspicions I share—I didn't feel I could face her and act as if everything was fine.

Edna and I picked a two-person table across the room from where Myrtle and Susannah were sitting, but I'd forgotten to check on the whereabouts of Andrew Winston. We'd barely taken our seats when he walked over from the next table.

"How dare you!" The words were clearly directed at me, since he had his back to Edna.

I clenched my hands in my lap and kept my lips pressed together. My heart pounded so loudly I could barely hear him.

"You're the reason that woman came round and accused me of criminal behavior. Well, let me tell you, I don't stand for bullying."

That woman? Of course. He had to be talking about Josephine. I should have known she wouldn't stop investigating just because I'd walked away in the middle. But Andrew accusing her of bullying was laughable, given he was standing over me, red-faced and shaking a finger.

He leaned in, and I leaned back.

"Stop that!" The speaker was Edna. She had stood and now she pushed herself between Andrew and me and faced him with clenched fists.

"You're the bully, Andrew Winston. And if you don't leave Lillian alone, I'll call the police."

"Because they know you so well," he said. "Yeah, I know all about your little 'brush' with the law. You're a thief, and I doubt the police would take anything you have to say seriously."

"You're wrong about that," Myrtle said, wheezing a bit as she planted her walker behind Andrew. "They would take it seriously. You see, the chief of police is a very good friend to all of us. So I suggest that you step away and leave my friends alone."

Between Edna and Myrtle, Andrew was hemmed in and couldn't step away even if he wanted to. I gestured at Myrtle to move. She nodded and shifted her walker, allowing Andrew to escape, something he did after treating each of us to a malevolent glare.

"You must come join Susannah and me," Myrtle said after Andrew returned to his table. "You can't possibly enjoy a meal sitting so close to that, that dibblefart."

I blinked in surprise. I had never heard Myrtle use a vulgarity before. But in this case, it was the nearly perfect one to use. She'd raised her voice on the word and Andrew heard, and gave her an additional glare along with a discreet middle finger.

She ignored him and, with one of her queenly looks, waited for us to join her for the march across the room. Edna and I led with Myrtle puffing in our wake. That is until she suddenly veered over to the podium set up for when we have a speaker.

She set her walker to the side and reached to flip the microphone on, banging it with her bracelets in the process. She always wears at least three on her right arm so that everything she says is punctuated with *ka-ching*s. The microphone screeched in protest, pulling everyone's attention to her and making my hearing aids chirp in protest.

Edna and I stopped walking and turned to look.

Myrtle tapped the microphone, something

that was totally unnecessary, and then she leaned toward it and began speaking.

"I'm sure those of you who weren't close enough to hear what just went on over there are wondering about it." She pointed toward where Edna and I had been sitting, banging the microphone yet again in the process. Then she looked around the room. Heads were nodding.

"That was just a little difference of opinion between Edna, Lillian, and me with Andrew Winston. But before I go into that, I have something else to say. I know that many of you are familiar with the rumor that recently circulated about my son." She stopped and took a shaky breath. "My son, who died in an accident on his wedding day, many years ago." Her voice trembled. She was obviously trying not to cry. Without complete success.

"It was a terrible tragedy for our family, and the worst day of my life." She stopped and pulled a tissue out of her pocket and mopped her eyes. "Someone started a rumor that he'd murdered someone. That wasn't true." She slapped the podium, making me jump. "And it was a cruel, cruel thing for someone to do." She sniffed, cleared her throat, and looked around the room. The servers were all frozen in place and every one of the residents was focused on her.

"Recently, a new rumor started making the rounds. It was about my very good friend, Lillian

Fitzel. And it was more than cruel. It was wicked. And there is absolutely no truth in it either. None!"

One of the women seated near the podium said, "Well, what was it?"

"I hesitate to even repeat it." Myrtle looked at me, and I knew it really didn't matter what I did, so I shrugged.

She repeated the rumor, keeping it brief, which surprised me. I had no idea Myrtle was capable of brevity.

"Oh, well, that's not good, is it," said the woman who'd asked about the rumor.

"Not only is it not good, let me repeat. It's. Not. True. And then, because of that rumor, a number of you were asked to sign a petition, asking the manager to kick Lillian out. And more than a few of you signed it."

She paused, taking a deep breath before continuing.

"You need to know, the person who seems most interested in pushing that petition forward is Andrew Winston. And he just confronted Lillian, right here in this room and called her the *b* word. Yes, ladies, you know the one I'm talking about. And all I can say, Andrew Winston, is who do you think you are?"

"Who's Andrew Winston?" The speaker was

the woman who'd earlier asked about the rumor. Her name is Aggie, and she tends to be both a little hard of hearing and insistent on making sure she does hear everything.

"He's right over there, Aggie," Myrtle said, pointing. "In the blue shirt. Perhaps you'd like to stand, Andrew? No? Well, we can all still see you."

"Oh, him," Aggie said. "He does look unpleasant, doesn't he?"

"Penis!" This time the speaker was Pru Parker, of course. The word echoed through the room, followed by titters. Andrew glared. Apparently his default reaction.

"Well, yes," Myrtle said. "He is definitely a man, Pru. One to steer clear of, in my opinion."

"I steer clear of 'em all," Pru said.

"We know you do, Pru," Myrtle said. "But if you and Aggie could let me finish?" Aggie made a zipping-her-lips motion, and Pru turned her back on the room. She sits at a table facing the wall so the men won't bother her, or she them.

"Now, for those of you who signed that petition, I will find out who you are and whether you do what I'm now going to suggest. First, you need to go see Marge and have your name removed. After that, I want you to take a few minutes to reflect on why you were so willing to sign such a document. Was it because Lillian is African American that you found it easy to think the worst of her?"

By this point, there was a growing level of murmurs throughout the room, and I wished the floor would open up and swallow me. Edna and I had been standing, but now we made our way to Myrtle's table and sat down.

Edna reached out and laid a hand on my arm. Then she tapped, and when I looked at her, she pointed. Marge, our manager, was standing at the entrance to the dining room, watching Myrtle with a bemused look.

"Okay then," Myrtle continued. "Once you've examined your consciences, I want you to make a point of getting to know Lillian better, and, if you can manage it, I want you to apologize to her. With sincerity."

Oh, no! The last thing I wanted was to have people ambushing me with fake apologies.

I tried to wave my hands at Myrtle, but she just waved back and smiled at me. She stood for a moment longer, looking around the room. Then, with a nod, she reached for her walker and made her way to our table. As she did that, Marge walked up to the podium.

"I want to thank Myrtle for such eloquent and important words in defense of her friend," Marge said, leading a round of applause.

"And I want to second everything she said."

She stopped and made eye contact with several people. She may have even looked at Andrew. "This is your home. And all of us in this room should act like family toward each other. That means we should avoid gossip and be, at the least, courteous and respectful toward each other. Even better, if we can manage it, we should be friendly and supportive. I've been very disturbed by the gossip making the rounds these last few days, and particularly disturbed by the direction that gossip recently took, in the form of a petition that some of you signed. I echo Myrtle in saying I would welcome you coming to me to remove your names. And I ask that if any of you hear disturbing gossip in the future, please come to me immediately. If you tell me what you heard and where you heard it, together we'll stamp out what is fast becoming a scourge on our community." She stopped and looked around the room. "That's all I have to say, since Myrtle said it so well. Enjoy your lunch."

"My goodness," Edna said. "That was . . ."

"Indeed it was," Susannah pitched in, when Edna couldn't seem to find the word she wanted.

"Well, it just had to be said, didn't it," Myrtle said, smoothing her napkin on her lap. "I hope it was okay with you, Lillian. I just couldn't stand by another minute without saying something."

My throat was so tight, I couldn't have spoken if my life depended on it, and so I nodded.

"I just hope they take me seriously and do what I asked," Myrtle said.

Inwardly, I shuddered at what she might have set loose.

"Well, it was a splendid effort on your part," Susannah said, smiling at Myrtle. "And I'm certain Lillian is grateful."

She looked at me, and I managed another nod.

"Well," Susannah said. "If we're done with that, I have news. I've adopted a sweet little kitty."

I realized I was blinking in surprise. Susannah has never struck me as the type to have a pet, although every witch does need a cat companion, I suppose.

The way her eyes sparkled as she talked about her new pet, I was suddenly uncertain she could be mean-spirited enough to be the source of the rumors.

"Ooh," Myrtle said, clasping her hands together. "Male or female?"

"A little female, of course."

"I want to meet her," Myrtle said.

Edna and I exchanged a glance before turning our attention to the salads that had just been placed in front of us.

"Maybe you can help me come up with a

name."

"I'd love that," Myrtle said.

Thankfully, for the rest of the lunch, Myrtle and Susannah talked about both past pets and Susannah's newest companion, leaving Edna and me in peace to pick at our food.

As soon as my plate was cleared, I excused myself and escaped back to my apartment. I badly needed a nap, but after that, I was calling Josephine.

Chapter Twelve

Josephine

Norman and I had already heard about Myrtle's star turn by the time I picked Lill up for dinner. We walked into the kitchen, still talking about it.

"My word, that woman," Lill said, but I didn't think she was truly upset. More like she was surprised at what Myrtle had done and maybe a teeny bit impressed and possibly also grateful.

"Marge said she was magnificent," Norman said, joining us in the kitchen. "She called me five minutes after it happened, chortling."

"Well, she wouldn't think it was so funny if

she were in my shoes."

"Has anyone recanted?" I asked.

"Oh, yes. A couple of people. It was quite an ordeal getting through their apologies, reassuring them they were forgiven, and then getting them to move on."

"Could they tell you any more about where they heard the rumor?"

"They didn't remember who told them. All they could remember was that Andrew was the one who pushed them to sign the petition."

The doorbell rang, and I went to answer. I knew who it would be, of course. I'd managed, finally, to get in touch with Glory and had invited her to join us for dinner. I was glad to discover she'd already talked to Lill and knew about the rumor. She came in and immediately made her way to Lill's side.

"Lill. I'm so sorry I wasn't here for you."

"How is your friend?" Lill said, greeting Glory with a worried look.

"Not good. It may not be long, so I need to get back as soon as possible."

"Of course you do," Lill said. "All this can wait."

Glory shook her head. "I'm here now. And I can stay a little while. I wanted to talk to you three, anyway, about why I'm at Brookside."

"That sounds intriguing," Norman said, taking a seat across from Glory and Lill.

"Okay. So here's the deal," Glory said. "I'm here because of my friend."

"The one who's so sick?" Lill asked.

"Yes. You see, a few months back, she let herself get talked into an investment by a couple living in her retirement community. A Roxanne and Chuck Carpenter. Chuck supposedly had an excellent reputation as a financial advisor. At least that was the way other residents viewed him. And the investment he proposed to Dorothy sounded good without sounding too good, if you know what I mean."

She paused, apparently gathering her thoughts. "Dorothy agreed to invest $10,000. Right after the deal was finalized, she experienced a setback and had to be hospitalized. Once she was home and began to check on her affairs, she discovered two withdrawals from her bank account by Carpenter Growth Associates. One was for $10,000, the second for $90,000. She figured it had to be a mistake."

"I'll say," Lill said.

"Anyway, she went to speak to Carpenter about it. He claimed that her agreement had been to buy 10,000 shares at the current price and not to a spending limit of $10,000. She then asked him to explain why there'd been two withdrawals, and his response was a word salad, but the bottom line was that the 10,000 shares cost $100,000."

"I make it a point never to believe word salad," I said, as Glory paused.

"And neither did Dorothy," Glory said. "So she asked for an accounting of what was happening with the stock. Carpenter stopped by a couple of days later with a set of documents indicating the company had gone bust."

"That's not good," Lill said.

"Dorothy was shocked, as you can imagine. When she questioned Carpenter further, he claimed she'd been fully informed that the investment was high risk since the potential reward was also high, and that he was sorry it hadn't worked out. Then he started to take the paperwork back, but Dorothy refused to give it to him. She told him to leave or she would pull her emergency cord. He left, and shortly after that, she called me." Glory paused again, but I think we all knew she had more to tell us.

"Dorothy has been a careful, cautious investor all her life. She never would have invested that much money in something that was presented to her as speculative, and especially not now when she's so ill. I haven't a single doubt that she agreed to invest $10,000, not ten times that."

"So, this wasn't just a case of buyer's remorse?" Norman said.

"Absolutely not. Dorothy's an honorable person. If the investment legitimately tanked, she'd accept that."

"What was the investment?" Lill asked.

"A company that has developed a revolutionary solar powered device for water purification that can be used in places like Africa and India. It was one of Dorothy's passions, you see. She'd previously made charitable contributions to help provide clean water to African communities, so investing in a start-up that might be able to provide a cheaper, more effective alternative to current systems seemed especially appealing to her. She did it more to help the company flourish than to make a profit."

"Would Carpenter have known that about her?" Norman asked.

Glory nodded. "Dorothy gave a talk about her efforts to help provide clean water to an African village a couple of weeks before Carpenter approached her."

"And Carpenter? Did you speak to him?"

Glory shook her head. "By the time Dorothy told me about this, he and his wife had moved out without leaving a forwarding address."

"So let me take a wild guess here," I said with a Myrtle-like flash of inspiration. "The Carpenters have now set up business at Brookside."

"They have. But they've changed their name to Culpepper."

Culpepper? Where had I heard that name before?

"Oh, I know them," Lill said. "He's a mousy little guy, and he goes by Charlie."

"He hasn't asked you to invest in anything, has he?" Glory said.

"Wouldn't do the man a bit of good," Lill said.

"I was hoping you were going to say it was the Winstons," I said. "We don't like him because he's the one behind the petition to get Lill kicked out of Brookside." I described my meeting with the man.

"You shouldn't have gone to see him on your own, Jo," Norman said, right on cue.

"I'm not sorry I did, though. And I wouldn't be a bit surprised to learn he was up to other nefarious activities."

"But Charlie Culpepper doesn't seem the nefarious type at all," Lill said. "Not that I'm actually acquainted with him."

"You said you needed our help," I said, turning to Glory and filing away the question of where I'd heard the Culpepper name before.

"I suspect this is a pattern for the Carpenters, now the Culpeppers," Glory said. "They move into a retirement community, get to know people, and then figure out how to part their fellow residents from their money. You see, they also got a couple of Dorothy's friends to invest, and their losses collectively were $30,000. They hadn't even realized the Carpenters had moved out and the money was gone until I talked to them."

"Do you know how long the Carpenters lived there?" Norman asked.

"Just under three months."

"So they were eligible to get their deposit back?"

I saw where he was going with his questions. Most retirement communities require a substantial up-front payment. In some cases, that payment is nonrefundable. In others, it can be fully or partially refunded if the person leaves or dies before a set amount of time has passed. The amount of time varies with the community. At Brookside, full refunds are possible within the first six months.

"They were within a week of losing their deposit, so that may have been the reason they left when they did," Glory said. "Although I suspect Dorothy confronting them may have also played a part."

"Did you go to the police?" Norman asked.

"We don't have evidence of an actual crime. After all, companies do fail and investors do lose all their money. But I've gone through the documents they gave Dorothy, and I'm positive that the company was fake, and that they took advantage of the fact she was ill. It made me mad enough that I want to stop them from doing it to anyone else."

"It's an expensive approach for a scam," Norman said. "Moving into a community."

"That may be," I said. "But if they pulled in $130,000 that quickly, that should more than cover their expenses."

"It could have been even more," Glory said. "I only checked with Dorothy's closest friends. There might be others who haven't yet noticed they've lost their money."

"You said the company was a fake?" Norman said.

"There's an African company with an almost identical name that appears to be both legitimate and still in business. And they manufacture water disinfection units. I suspect the Carpenters were counting on investors who checked on the internet to miss the slight difference in the spelling of the name or to assume there was a typo in the paperwork. Dorothy said Carpenter showed her a slick paper prospectus with excellent financials before she invested."

"All created out of whole cloth," Norman said.

"It certainly appears so."

"Do you have proof the Carpenters are now

the Culpeppers?"

"Here, let me show you." Glory opened her purse and pulled out a sheaf of photographs. "These were taken at social events. Dorothy's friends located them for me."

The three of us shared them out and examined them.

I didn't recognize the Culpeppers, but Lill did. She pointed them out to me.

"How did you find out they were here?" Lill asked.

"I made a list of communities with a liberal grace period for refunding the initial payment. Then I had a friend visit, saying he was an attorney trying to get in touch with a potential heir. That he didn't know the woman's married name, but he had photos. Once I learned the Carpenters were here and had changed their names to Culpepper, I decided to take up temporary residence myself to see if I could catch them in the act."

"And have you?" Lill asked.

"It's trickier than I thought it would be to cozy up to people and ask about their finances," Glory said. "That's why, now that I've gotten to know you three, I've decided to ask for your help. I suspect they tailor their approach depending on what they find out about a person. In Dorothy's case, I think their initial plan was hatched to focus on her interest in water purification. And a commitment of ten thousand was probably a win. But when they realized how ill she was, I think they decided they could take a chance on transferring more funds than she'd agreed to. And if she hadn't told me about it, the loss might never have been noticed."

"You mean because she's dying," I said.

"Yes. In the case of her two friends, only the agreed-upon amount was transferred."

"I'm guessing it's all in the Caymans by now," Norman said.

"I'm afraid so," Glory said.

"So, did they target Dorothy first, and then, based on her participation, go after her friends?"

"I think so. Both friends said the Carpenters mentioned Dorothy's investment."

"Well, if we start with the assumption they're planning to do something similar here, who do we think they might pick?" I said.

"What about the Winstons?" Norman said.

"The Winstons do seem to have struck up a friendship with the Culpeppers," Glory said. "But they may not have their hooks into anyone yet. They've been here only a month. And they can take their time since they have six months to set things up. So will you help me stop them from taking anybody else's money?"

"Of course," Lill and I said together.

"You know, we might just be able to do more than stop them," Norman said. "I think we ought to consider coming up with a way to con them out of their ill-gotten gains. Maybe we can even recover what they stole from your friend."

"How would you do that?" Glory asked.

"At the moment, I have no idea. But I'm betting Richard will be able to come up with something," Norman said.

"Richard?" Glory said. "Philippa's Richard?"

"He's an ex-con man," I said.

"My goodness. Brookside is simply awash in dodgy characters."

"It is. And there isn't even a brook," Lill said.

"Richard has mended his ways," Norman said. "Now he consults with the police, but I doubt he'd say no to a little side caper."

"He was certainly willing to help Lill and me con a murderer into confessing," I said.

"Oh," Glory said, blinking rapidly and turning toward Lill. "I have to confess, I thought that was a tall tale you were spinning me."

"Whatever Lill told you was true," I said. "If anything, it was probably the vanilla version."

"Someday, you'll have to give me the chocolate one, then," Glory said.

"Definitely. Say, why don't I call Richard and Philippa and invite them to come over after dinner?"

"And I'll get dinner on the table now," Norman said. "Tell them we'll be ready for them about seven."

~ ~ ~

"You wanted to consult with us about something?" Richard asked once we were all seated in the living room with either tumblers of elderly Scotch or cups of tea in front of us.

Norman summarized what Glory had told us.

"So, you want to come up with an investment scheme even better than the one Culpepper is probably working on as we speak."

"Exactly," Glory said.

"Well, if we're going to land them, I'm going to need all of you to help."

"You have something in mind?" I said.

"A few random ideas is all. But it would be really helpful to know if they've approached anybody yet. Do you have any thoughts about that?" Richard asked.

"I've been watching who they've been interacting with," Glory said. "I'd say in addition to the Winstons, the other possibilities are the two ladies with the colored hair."

"The Frosties," I said. "AKA Martha and Mary Spear. I just spoke to them this morning.

Nothing came up about any investment, but they did take a swipe at each other over the petition. And then one of them made a comment about another snap decision. You know, I believe they mentioned Culpepper. It wasn't clear what it was about, though. But it might be an iffy investment."

"Definitely worth checking," Richard said. "Do you mind asking them about it, Jo?"

"Happy to. Why don't I give them a call right now?" I went into the kitchen to make the call, since the living room was full of people. I got the number from the front desk. The phone rang seven times, and I was about to hang up when it was answered.

"This is Josephine Neuman. I stopped by to talk to you this morning. Is this Martha or Mary?" I asked.

"Oh, we're both on the line. When we saw your name pop up on caller ID, we had a bit of a tussle to decide who should answer, until we remembered the second phone."

"Good that you're both on, because I have a question for you both."

"Is it about that petition? Because I fully intend to apologize to Lillian, and I already had my name removed." That had to be Mary.

"Not exactly. What I wanted to ask about was, well, this will sound odd, but have either of you talked to Charlie Culpepper about a possible investment?"

"Oh, my, indeed we have. But how did you know about that?"

The second voice cut in. "My goodness, Josephine. You are on top of all the gossip, aren't you? Although, investment is not precisely correct."

"No, no. He called it a guaranteed something or other."

"A GIL. Guaranteed Income for Life. That's the term he used. All we have to do is buy a GIL policy for twenty-five thousand dollars, and we'll be guaranteed a monthly income of one thousand dollars for life. Even if we live more than twenty-five months, something we fully intend to do, don't we Martha."

"Have you given him the money yet?"

"We're going to."

"We haven't quite decided." Their voices overlapped, and I let out a breath of relief. I was in time.

"Can I ask you a favor?"

"Of course."

"What is it?" Again, the voices overlapped.

"Can you delay the decision about this?"

"Well, he did say the offer was only good until the end of the year. After that he couldn't guarantee the payout would be anywhere near a thousand a month."

"But that means you still have fifteen days. Give me five of them, okay?"

"I don't suppose five more days will make a difference."

"Well, I don't think Charlie's going to be happy about it. I think we should just go ahead."

I wished I could sort out which voice was which, but with the rapid exchanges, they sounded too much alike. I decided to plunge in. "So here's the thing. Mary, I think both you and Martha should be completely on board before doing something this consequential, and it sounds like one of you is hesitating. Am I right?"

"You are. I think we need to give this more thought, and you know that, Mary."

Good, I now knew that Martha was the one who was less gung ho. "Martha's right, Mary. You want to be completely sure before you do something like this. And if you give me five days, I'll be able to tell you if this is an excellent idea or one you should run from. That's all I'm asking. Some time to make sure you make the best decision for the two of you."

"Why?" one of the voices queried. "It seems odd to me that you're suddenly calling out of the blue and questioning our investment decisions."

My mind whirled, trying to come up with a reason. The last thing I wanted was for them to tell Culpepper I'd called and asked them to wait.

Okay, I had it.

"Here's the thing. Charlie approached Lill about something similar, and she asked me to check into it. And then it occurred to me from our discussion this morning that he might've asked you as well, and, well, I just want to be sure it's all okay for the three of you."

There was a moment of silence.

"Please?" I said. "It would really set my mind at ease to be able to check on things. But you can't tell Charlie that I've asked you to delay."

"Well, what should we tell him, then?"

"How about—"

"Oh, it's simple, Martha. Christmas is coming. We can just say Christmas is a big deal for us, and we simply can't decide until it's over. But we'll definitely let him know before New Year's."

"That sounds good," I said. "The simpler you keep it, the better."

"Okay, Josephine. You'll let us know what you find out?"

"I certainly will. And you'll let me know if Charlie gives you a hard time?"

"We will."

"But please don't mention my name."

They agreed, and sighing with relief, I ended the call. We now had the confirmation we needed that the Carpenter-Culpeppers were pulling scams at Brookside like they'd previously pulled on Dorothy and her friends, and that was all we needed at the moment.

"Glory's right about why the Culpeppers are here," I said, when I returned to the living room. "The Frosties were within an argument or two of signing over twenty-five thousand dollars for a GIL—Guaranteed Income for Life—plan. I got them to agree to delay until after Christmas. But Charlie did tell them they needed to sign up before the end of the year, or the deal wouldn't be nearly as good."

"Of course he did," Lill said. "Classic sales pressure. I just wish we knew if there were any others who need saving."

"Well, you, for one," I said. "I told the Frosties you'd also been approached, and that was why I was checking with them."

"It's good to have that information," Richard said. "But we better not ask around anymore. Word might filter through to Roxanne and Charlie, and that would be that."

"So, what comes next?" I asked.

He raised a finger. "Still thinking." After several minutes of silence that the rest of us filled with glances and sips of our respective beverages, he spoke. "I have an idea, and you know who might be the perfect person to suck the Culpeppers in?"

Nobody ventured a guess.

"Myrtle Grabinowitz."

There was a moment of surprised silence.

"So, what would you have her do?" Lill said. "Pretend she has lots of money? Tell Charlie she's heard he's a financial wizard and she wants in on the action?"

"Nothing quite that obvious," Richard said.

"If you're trying to avoid being obvious, Myrtle is definitely not your girl," Lill said.

"But in this situation, her brand of drama might be just what's needed," Richard said.

"So, Myrtle is your secret sauce?" Norman said.

"That may be the perfect description," Richard said.

"You know Myrtle," Lill said. "You say sauce, she hears star."

"You might be better off not letting her know she's the star," I said. "Or the sauce, for that matter."

Richard started to speak, then stopped, got a thoughtful look, and began nodding. "That's an excellent point, Jo. What I have in mind might work even better with Myrtle only partly clued in."

"There could be unintended consequences," I warned.

"Or maybe, with only partial information,

she'll come across as more normal," Philippa offered.

"Myrtle would rather die than be considered merely normal," Lill said.

"I almost have it," Richard said, eyes narrowed. "Let me get a few things in place, and then we'll have another talk, but what we're going for is a little scene between Myrtle, Lill, and, yes, Edna, I think." He pursed his lips, still planning.

"By the way, do you think the Culpeppers could be the source of the rumor about Lill?" I asked Glory, leaving Richard to his cogitations.

"I doubt it," Richard said, suddenly alert. "If they're planning what we think they are—a wholesale scam of Brookside residents—they wouldn't have a thing to gain from something like that."

"So, maybe we have more than one villain," Lill said, rubbing her hands together.

"Indeed," Glory said. "So what are we going to do about the *rumormonger...er?*"

"Catch her, put her in a cage, and poke her with sticks," Lill said with a grin.

I couldn't blame her for being just a teeny bit bloodthirsty.

Maybe while Richard did his plotting, Lill and I could do some plotting of our own.

Chapter Thirteen

Myrtle

Well, of course I can act. I don't know why Richard would hesitate even a microsecond, whatever that is, before asking me. It's something Josephine said once, and I remember it because it was rather odd. "Don't worry about that for a microsecond."

Anyway, what he's suggesting is so easy, I could do it with my eyes closed. I need to keep them open, of course. I wouldn't want to miss any of the action, not to mention I might bang into someone with my walker, and that would ruin the whole effect.

It's such a pain having to use a walker, but it has made it easier for me to get around, and when I get tired, I can stop and sit for a while since it has its own built-in seat. Such a clever invention. I bet I could even ice skate with it. I'm not going to, I assure you, but it's rather nice to know that I could.

Richard was terribly vague about why he needs us to do this *skit*, as he calls it. And by us I mean Lillian, Edna, and me. I have the most important role. Naturally. Since I'm the only one who's been on the stage. And for more than a microsecond, I assure you.

Anyway, I couldn't get a straight answer about why we're doing this, just some mumbly pumbly that it's an idea he's working on that he wants to try out. And that might mean a road show.

Goodie, goodie. I can just see us going around and performing for other retirement communities, like we did before. I helped with that, too. Naturally.

And don't think I didn't notice that Josephine wasn't asked to be part of this. I hope it didn't put her nose out of joint. Of course, she rarely eats in the dining room anymore, so it might look odd if she were here. I'm supposed to be sure to mention her name, though. So I don't see why she couldn't just be here. But then, if she were there, she'd try to take charge. So it's better this way.

Although, maybe, I'll just put on my thinking cap and see if I can't come up with some additions to jazz things up a bit. Bottom line, it's about time someone recognized my talent.

Chapter Fourteen

Lillian

Oh, my. Clearly, we should've had someone supervise Myrtle's choice of clothing for our little charade. Although if the point was for her to be the center of attention, she's certainly achieved that. She's pushing her walker toward us, wearing a purple top that glitters with . . . rhinestones? Very sixties, I would have said. Appropriate for a rock concert. Of course, Myrtle would have been a bit long in the tooth for a rock concert in the sixties, but that's definitely the vibe. And worn by an eighty something-year-old woman for a weekday lunch at Brookside, it's—

"My goodness," Edna said, lifting her napkin to her lips. "That's quite, quite . . ."

"It certainly is," I said.

"Tu la ru. Lillian, Edna. I'm so glad you're here. I have such good news."

Myrtle has one of those voices that carry, and today she had raised it even further, and residents in every part of the dining room looked up or turned their heads to watch her progress across the room to our table. But then, that was the point, after all.

As she approached, she remembered the envelope sticking out of her tote. She reached for it with one hand, propelling the walker forward with the other.

I closed my eyes, expecting disaster.

"Oopsy daisy."

I opened my eyes to see Myrtle leaning precariously to the left, the right hand waving the envelope, bracelets kicking up a storm. Luckily, the walker had snagged against a chair, briefly stopping Myrtle's momentum, and one of the more alert servers made a dive, managing to prop Myrtle back up. He rescued the walker as well and reunited it with Myrtle.

She gave him her queenly look with a "Thank you, young man." Then she brushed her hair out of her eyes, forgetting she was holding the envelope. She shook her head as if warding off a fly, then stood for a moment, obviously trying to remember what she was supposed to be doing. I held my breath, thinking the whole thing was done for. If this had been a rehearsal, Richard would undoubtedly have stepped in by now and yelled CUT.

She re-settled her hands on the walker's handlebars, the envelope being scrunched in the process, and moved tentatively away from the table that had saved her from disaster. Moving much more carefully, she continued toward us. The server who'd saved the day followed behind and helped move the walker out of the way so she could take a seat. She settled with an, "Oomph," and gave us both a triumphant look.

"Remember the envelope," I whispered. She was clutching it, but had clearly forgotten what she needed to do next.

"Oh, sorry." She took a moment to catch her breath.

"What is it, Myrtle?" I said, speaking loudly and distinctly. "You seem excited about something." I was trying to redeem the situation, but I have to admit I don't have Myrtle's flair.

She glared at me, and I tapped her foot under the table, trying to get her to focus. Maybe I needn't bother. Maybe this scene was already so far out of control, we just needed to scrap it and try something else. The Culpeppers had already stopped watching us and were checking their menu cards.

"I have news," Myrtle said, still slightly out of breath, but remembering to raise her voice, making my hearing aids squawk. She pulled the papers out of the envelope and waved them at us.

"Well, for Pete's sake, what is it?" Edna said, also speaking louder than she normally did, but still managing to sound completely herself.

"It's that investment *Josephine* suggested. It's already gone up *nine percen*t, and she says that's only the beginning. The sky's the limit. This is just so exciting," Myrtle said in that rock-slicing voice.

I saw the Culpeppers look over at us, and I was pretty sure they were now riveted on our every word. I grabbed the paper out of Myrtle's hand.

"Where?" I asked. "Show me."

"Right there." Myrtle pointed at a vague location in the middle of the sheet, and I pretended to look at it. I had to hold the paper out and tip my head in order to see the numbers. It was all gobbledygook, but I know Richard worked hard on it.

"And all I can say, Lillian, is that if you don't invest something too, well, you're just being really shortsighted. It's like backing a fifty-to-one long shot at the track and watching it cross the finish line first. And you don't want to miss out on that!"

Whoa. Myrtle was definitely getting carried away. But it was working. The Culpeppers weren't even trying to pretend they weren't listening.

"Let me see," Edna said, taking the papers from me. "Well, I can't make heads or tails of this, but nine percent you said? That's good, right? If I had two nickels to rub together, you know I'd be right there with you. Lillian, you really need to reconsider."

"I've already talked to *Josephine* about this, and I'd need a lot more than two nickels in order to invest," I said, making sure I was projecting toward the Culpeppers.

"So what are we going to do to celebrate Myrtle's good fortune?" Edna aimed that last bit at me, with a glint of the devil in her eye. Since we hadn't practiced any specific lines, I knew she was messing with me.

"How about we go out for ice cream," I said, giving her a *so there* look.

"Oh, that would be lovely," Myrtle said. "I expect we can get *Josephine* to take us."

"I'll ask her," I said.

Edna handed the papers to Myrtle. She stuffed them back into the envelope and laid that next to her plate with a pat. Then she leaned in and whispered as loudly as she could manage, and that was loud enough for everyone within a twenty-foot radius, including the Culpeppers, to hear. "We really need to keep this to ourselves, you know. *Josephine* would be very upset if we spread it around."

"Well, you're the one making a big deal of it," Edna whispered back.

"Well, I never. You could be nicer, Edna."

Myrtle sat back and settled into her seat, and Edna looked properly chastened.

The server arrived at that point to deliver our salads, and may I just say, I was relieved we were done with the play-acting. It's exhausting.

Myrtle stifled a grin by taking a sip of water. I'm quite certain she thought her performance had been outstanding. Well, it had certainly captured and held the attention of the Culpeppers, and that had been our most important assignment. Now all that was left to do was for Myrtle to knock the envelope under the table as we were leaving. We'd talked about it and decided that would be better than leaving it on the table where one of the servers was sure to scoop it up and return it to Myrtle before we made it out of the room. Myrtle didn't know what was supposed to happen to the envelope after that, but I did. It was the bait.

The only problem was that the Culpeppers had already been served their main course and would probably finish before us, and that meant they might very well walk out before the envelope made it under the table.

"We need to eat faster," I said, leaning in so I could speak softly.

"What are you talking about?" Myrtle said. "It's not a good idea to eat quickly. It can give you gas."

"We're going to have to skip dessert, then," I

said.

"Oh, no, we can't skip dessert," Myrtle said. "It's the only reason I eat salad. My doctor told me, no dessert unless I eat my salad, and as you can see, I've eaten my salad."

"Myrtle," I said, "stop talking."

She did.

"Here's the thing. I'll ask someone to package a dessert for you if you'll eat a little faster."

"You still haven't said why. Do you know something I don't know? Yes. Yes, you do. Lillian, you sly dog. What is it?"

"Please, keep your voice down," I said. "Here's the deal. You're supposed to leave the envelope behind, right? And that's so someone will pick it up. But that someone won't be able to pick it up if they've already left the room."

"Who? Who's the someone, Lillian. I know you know," Myrtle said.

"I'll tell you later. Promise."

"Oh, okay. But you have to get me a dessert," Myrtle said.

"Fine. I'll do that right now, while you finish eating."

"All right," Myrtle said.

Throughout this conversation, I'd been keeping an eye on the Culpeppers. They were sitting with the Winstons, and the four of them had been chatting and were no longer paying any attention to us. Thank goodness.

I left the table in search of a server to request the to-go dessert and then I returned and got Edna and Myrtle moving. Myrtle did an excellent job of knocking the envelope under the table as the server was helping her with her walker. Then the three of us left together.

"Where's my dessert?" Myrtle asked as we reached the doorway.

I handed it to her and glanced over at where Richard was sitting in the lounge area. He gave me a discreet thumbs up. I hoped that meant we'd done okay.

"Now, Lillian, exactly when are we going out for that ice cream?" Myrtle said.

~ ~ ~

As we sat down at one of the tiny tables at Aglamesis with our ice creams, Myrtle leaned toward Josephine and me. "Was he watching, do you think?"

"Who?"

"Andrew, of course. He's the baddie, am I right?"

Of course he wasn't, but she was warm. "Good guess," I said.

"Yes. I thought so." She licked some

raspberry ripple ice cream off her spoon, looking very satisfied with herself.

"Did he fall for it?" I asked Josephine. I figured Richard would have reported immediately.

"Oh, yes. It was picked up slick as you please," Josephine said, winking at me. She knew that I knew she was talking about Charlie Culpepper, not Andrew Winston.

"Well, I should hope so," Myrtle said. "I think we were amazing, except for Lillian. That one line of yours was definitely stiff."

"And you almost lost the plot and took out that table," I shot back. Although she was right about my sounding stiff, I was still the one who'd saved the whole thing from disaster.

"Richard said all three of you were brilliant," Josephine said. It was an obvious attempt to smooth the waters, and after a brief hesitation, I sat back and focused on my butter pecan ice cream instead of my grievances.

Chapter Fifteen

Myrtle

My goodness, what an eventful day I've had. There was the performance at lunch that was, in my opinion, a great success. And then there was the celebration at Aglamesis afterward. So much going on, I almost missed my nap.

Now, the only thing missing is the full briefing Richard promised, once he saw if his ploy worked. I'm quite certain the target was Andrew Winston, and I'm looking forward to finding out what Richard suspects Andrew of, besides being a thoroughly unpleasant person.

Of course Josephine no doubt knows the whole story, but she changed the subject every time I asked her about it. I do believe I'm owed an explanation after playing such an important role in whatever Richard's scheme is. I can see now that I should've demanded to know what it was all about before doing the dirty deed.

I wonder if Lillian knows the full story. Probably, since she and Josephine are so tight. And may I just say that Lillian had no business scolding me for losing focus when she was the one who delivered her lines like a robot and almost nixed the whole thing. And for the record, I did not lose focus—my balance, very briefly, but not my focus. Besides, didn't I pull it all together at the end, by making sure the envelope landed in Andrew Winston's direction? So stick that in your pipe and smoke it, Lillian Fitzel.

~ ~ ~

I'd just gotten up from my nap and was making myself a cup of tea when there was a knock on my door. I answered it to find Roxanne Culpepper standing there. Now that was a surprise. I don't believe the woman has ever even spoken to me before. And neither has her husband. A couple of cold fish, if you ask me. Or is it fishes? Anyway, if I'd tried to guess who was knocking before I answered the door, I would have been off by a mile.

"Myrtle, I'm so glad I caught you. I think you dropped this at lunch." She held out a suspiciously familiar envelope.

I'm quite sure this wasn't part of Richard's plan, but I ask you, what could I do but accept it?

"Why thank you."

"We heard you talking at lunch, and we were intrigued. It sounds like you've gotten some very good news."

Since Richard gave me no instructions of what to do if someone returned the envelope, I was on my own. I trotted out a smile. "That's so nice of you to return this." Then inspiration struck. "I'm just making a cup of tea. Would you like to join me?"

"Why, I'd love to. You know, Charlie and I were just saying we would love to get to know you better."

I know everybody thinks a compliment melts my brain. But I'm not stupid. If Charlie and Roxanne really wanted to get to know me, why had they completely ignored me up to now? I couldn't even remember them nodding and smiling when I encountered them in the hall. So this sudden interest in me raised my intuition hackles considerably. After all, why hadn't she simply turned the envelope in at the office instead of going to all the trouble of returning it personally? And how did she end up with it? It was supposed to go to the Winstons. I definitely smelled a rat.

I motioned Roxanne to a seat and went and finished making the tea, and then I joined her.

"My, you have quite the Precious Moments collection," she said.

"Indeed. One of my granddaughters gave me a piece when she was six. And of course I said it was my favorite gift of all time. She's now grown up, but she hasn't stopped. She said she intends to make sure I have the entire collection. I do think they're quite nice, although I would be just as happy with a BonBonerie opera crème cake."

"Oh, I know what you mean. Grandchildren. They're so wonderful, though."

"How many do you have?" I asked. I'm always happy to talk about grandchildren.

"Only one, so far, I'm afraid."

"A boy or a girl?"

"Oh, a little boy."

"Boys are grand, but there's nothing like a sweet little granddaughter. Or great-granddaughter." I've lived long enough to have a great-great-grandchild, although I'm not admitting that to Roxanne, who doesn't look a day over sixty-five.

"I bet you spoil them rotten," Roxanne said.

"Oh, I do."

"So, it's just terrific that you had such a nice windfall today."

"A windfall?"

"Your investment." She pointed at the envelope I'd laid on the coffee table. "We heard you talking about it."

"Oh, yes. My investment." It took me a moment to refocus from thinking about my grandchildren. "Well, today was nice, of course. But really, I've been doing extremely well investment-wise ever since I started taking Josephine and Richard's advice." I have no idea why I said that about Richard. It just slipped out.

"I don't believe I know a Richard or a Josephine. Do they live here?"

"Josephine used to live just down the hall. But then she got married. To Norman Neuman. And now they live in one of the new houses. They're wonderful friends of mine, you know."

"And Richard?"

"Yes. Richard. He's so clever. I mean, between the two of them, my investments have just grown and grown."

"Even during the downturn?"

"Yes. They told me to just hang on, and I did, and everything is coming back up very nicely." I had no idea what I was talking about, of course. But I had heard Josephine make a comment once about not getting out of the market when it was down because all that did was lock in losses. That makes sense, actually.

"How lovely for you." Roxanne took a sip of tea. "My, this tea is delicious."

"Josephine is quite the tea aficionado, among other things, and this was a gift from her."

"And this is the same Josephine who suggested the investment that's doing so well for you?"

"That's right." And trust me, my curiosity

hackles were staying nicely raised by the way she kept working in references to the investment. It seems that Richard's little plan has roped in the wrong interested party. Well, I guess I'll leave him to sort that out. But I may as well make the most of what's before me.

"Josephine is an investing wizard. You've probably heard about her Edward Hopper painting?"

"No, I don't believe so. Edward Hopper, you say?"

"His paintings are valued in the millions. Josephine bought hers a number of years ago, so she didn't pay millions, but that's what it's worth now."

"You mean to tell me she has a painting worth millions just hanging in her home?"

I was watching Roxanne carefully, and I had the distinct impression she was quite excited about what I was saying.

"Of course not. It's at the art museum. But that just gives you an idea of the resources Josephine has at her disposal since she can afford to donate a painting worth millions to the art museum."

"That's certainly impressive," Roxanne said, her eyes bulging slightly. I do believe that's a sign she's interested, not that she has a thyroid condition. Well, perhaps both are true.

"How do you like living here?" I asked, deciding I'd leave her to chew over what I'd told her about Josephine. And I do believe Richard would approve of the tactic. I'm not so sure Josephine would, though.

"Oh, we love it. We've already made wonderful new friends, and I'm hoping I can add you to that list?"

"You mean like Andrew Winston?" I said, ignoring the invitation to be her friend. I pick my friends more carefully than that.

She tittered. "Oh no, I can't stand the Winstons. But we can't seem to shake them. You were absolutely right about Andrew, you know. What you said the other day. Your friend Lillian seems like a lovely woman, and what Andrew did, well, it wasn't nice, was it."

"Certainly not. You really don't like him?"

"Of course not. He's a horrible man."

That made me warm to her, and I opened my mouth to tell her the financial statement was a ploy, but then I remembered that as I'd waited for Richard to give me the high sign to join Edna and Lillian today, I'd noticed, without realizing I was noticing, that the Winstons were already seated, and it was Roxanne and Charlie who decided to join them. If what Roxanne was saying was true, why hadn't she steered Charlie to another table?

I know that Josephine and Lillian think I'm gullible, and maybe even a bit silly. And perhaps I am. After all, I do like to think the best of everyone, and that isn't something one can say about Josephine. But you don't raise five children without developing a sixth sense when something peculiar is going on.

So, instead of cluing Roxanne in that the investment ploy was just that, a ploy, I set my tea down and checked my watch.

"Oh my, is it that time already? I need to get ready for dinner, but I do appreciate you stopping by and returning my property." I stood, and so, after a pause, did Roxanne. I walked her to the door, and as soon as she was through it, I pulled out my phone and called Richard.

Chapter Sixteen

Josephine

"And you saw him actually pick it up?" Norman asked. The five of us—Norman, Richard, Philippa, Lill and I—were holding a strategy session following the attempt to suck the Culpeppers into Richard's Amazing Investment

Opportunity. Glory was still with her dying friend.

"Not exactly. Myrtle knocked the envelope more in Andrew Winston's direction, but that worked out since he shared it with the Culpeppers."

"Myrtle made one of her leaps of illogic and settled on Andrew as the villain," Lill said.

"She told you that?"

"On the way out. She may not be right, but she's rarely uncertain, and she always has a theory."

"Five children," I said.

Richard raised his eyebrows.

"Well, that's Glory's theory," I said. "And personally, I think it's a better explanation than anything we've managed to come up with."

"Well, she was wrong this time," Richard said.

"But she was close to being right," I insisted. "Close enough the information got where it needed to go. Into the hands of the Culpeppers."

"I guess I'll have to grant her that."

"So has the JLR fund gotten any phone calls from prospective clients lately?" Norman asked.

Richard's phone rang, and he raised a finger to halt the discussion. He glanced at the phone, then at all of us. "It's Myrtle."

"Maybe put her on speaker?" Lill said.

It was clear from the first few words that

Myrtle was excited. "You'll never guess who just came to see me," she said. Then without drawing a breath, " Roxanne Culpepper."

Myrtle hardly ever gives anyone a chance to guess, so when she says, "You'll never guess who or what," mostly we don't bother to try. And she was correct this time. I doubt that Roxanne would have been on any list Lill and I came up with.

"Just like that? She came to see you?" Richard said.

"To return the envelope," Myrtle said.

Richard's shoulders tensed.

"She did natter on about my good fortune, though, so I'm positive she looked at the papers. I made sure she knew you and Josephine were the ones who helped me and that Josephine is simply amazing at investing. I hope that was okay. I mean, I expect she'll share what I said with the Winstons. That's what you wanted, right? Besides, you didn't tell me what to do if they asked me more questions, so I had to improvise. Oh, and I told her about Josephine's painting."

I really, really hate it when Myrtle starts telling new residents all she thinks she knows about me. None of it is a secret, but if she would just stop bringing it up, pretty soon new people would never hear the stories, and those who'd already heard them would eventually forget them. The same is true for Edna. The people who were here at the time of her transgressions have either died or forgotten what she did. Without Myrtle and the phantom poster, Edna and I would have sunk into comfortable anonymity by now. As for Myrtle bringing up Richard's name, well, that's probably a good thing.

"And here's the thing," Myrtle continued. "Besides asking all those questions about my windfall, she said she and Charlie really want to be my friends, even though neither one of them has ever spoken to me before. So, if you think I found her whole visit suspicious, you'd be right. She even said she despised the Winstons, although I find that hard to believe since they sit together all the time."

Myrtle paused to catch her breath, and I realized I needed to take a breath as well.

"And you did say you'd let me know what it was all about and who the real villain was, but you haven't. I'm guessing Andrew Winston. Am I right? Although, in that case, it's maybe not good that Roxanne was the one who returned the envelope. I'm going to have to give that some more thought."

We all exchanged looks. The last thing any of us wanted was for Myrtle to think.

"As a matter of fact—" Richard said.

"So I just wanted you to know that I tried not to mess things up. That was difficult since you didn't tell me everything. And may I just say that when Roxanne said she despised Andrew, I almost told her it was all a setup to catch him in the act of . . . something. But then I realized that might not be the best thing. After all, she may say she despises Andrew, but she doesn't act like she does. So I just kept my lips zipped about all that and let her talk."

If Myrtle was this chatty with Roxanne, I very much doubted the other woman got many words in edgewise.

"But you do owe me the full story."

"You're right, I do," Richard said. "Actually, I'm checking out both the Winstons and the Culpeppers, so can I ask you to be careful what you say to any of them?"

"Oh, indeed you can. Not a word. You don't have to worry about Andrew and his wife, of course. They make a point of glaring at me any time I get close to them. So I don't think I'll be talking to either of them. As for the Culpeppers, if Roxanne shows up again, I'll just say my friend quota is currently filled to the brim, so I'm very, very sorry, but I'll just have to decline their kind offer until there's an opening. How does that sound?"

"Perfect," Richard said, shaking his head.

After a few more exchanges, Richard finally managed to end the call.

He looked up as he pocketed his phone.

"Sounds like the plan had a close call there," Norman said.

"Or maybe the hook went in just a little farther," Richard said. "Although, I'll admit having one of them return the envelope to Myrtle was a move I should have anticipated."

"Well, no harm done," Lill said. "Apparently."

"So now all we can do is wait to see how they react?" I asked.

"You might want to prepare yourself, Jo," Richard said.

"For what?"

"You heard Myrtle singing your praises. I think it's likely you're going to very shortly be making the acquaintance of Charlie and Roxanne Culpepper."

"That isn't the plan, is it?"

"Plans sometimes need to change due to circumstances."

"Oh, I like it," said Lill. "A new title for Myrtle: Ms. Changed Circumstances."

"What do I do if they contact me?" I asked.

"Make a date and bring me along," Richard said.

"You think it's going to work?" Lill asked.

"It's hard to con an honest man. Easy to con a dishonest one. Especially one who's also greedy."

The doorbell rang, and Norman and I exchanged questioning looks. I decided it was probably Glory and went to answer.

"I hope you don't mind," Devi said. "I know I should have called ahead. It's just, it was a last-minute decision to come over. I need your advice, you see."

"You know you're welcome any time." I drew her inside, where the murmur of voices could be heard.

"Oh, you have company. I'm so sorry. I'll come back another time."

It was so unusual for Devi to show up like this that there was no way I was letting her go without explaining the reason for her visit.

"It's just Lill, Philippa, and Richard," I said. "But if this is private, we can go to the den."

"Oh, no. That's okay. Maybe they can help, actually."

After greetings were exchanged, Devi took a seat and gave us all a worried look.

"You haven't talked to Mac lately, have you?" she asked.

We all shook our heads.

"So it's something to do with Mac?" I asked, with a sinking feeling.

"Sort of. Do any of you belong to one of those neighborhood email sites?"

Again, we all shook our heads.

"What is it, Devi?" I asked, feeling mystified.

"Someone's posted on a Montgomery site that Mac and I are living way beyond our means. They included a picture of the house and said it's worth nearly two million dollars, which I expect it is. And people have responded saying it's terrible to have a dishonest police chief and something should be done."

While she was speaking, Norman disappeared briefly before returning, carrying a laptop.

"What's the name of the site?" he asked, sitting down and opening the computer.

She told him.

"Do you have a sign-in name and password?"

Devi shook her head in frustration. "I don't. I mean, I do, but I can't remember it."

"That's okay. I'll just create an account."

While he did that, I filled Devi in on what had been happening at Brookside.

"There. Got it," Norman said. "Let me just check it out." After a minute, he looked up. "It appears the original post has been removed, but someone has posted about seeing it, and that its removal is just another sign of corruption."

"Mac did say the city's lawyer was going to contact the site to have it taken down. But the last time I checked it was still there, and there were over thirty comments. A few said he ought to be given a chance to respond, but most jumped on the bandwagon saying he should be investigated or removed."

"We can try posting," Norman said.

He started typing while we watched him.

"Here, how about this?"

I'm a Montgomery resident, and I'm personally acquainted with Police Chief McElroy. I happen to know that he and his wife are currently house-sitting while the owners of the home are spending a year in Italy. I'm quite certain the owners would be appalled to learn that Chief McElroy's reputation is being called into question by someone unacquainted with the facts.

"Sounds good," Richard said. "How about I set up an account and post something similar?"

"Can't hurt," Norman agreed, pressing ENTER.

"You can do one for me as well," Lill said. "You'll have to set it up, though. And type the post."

"Okay. That's three," Norman said. "Have you told Maddie about it?"

"I did. We didn't think about doing posts, though."

"Maybe ask her to do one as well?" I said.

Devi nodded. "I'm sure she'll do it. You really think it will work?"

"There are still going to be people who've seen the original post and won't see our comments, or maybe they won't believe our comments, but this should be some help," Richard said.

"You know, this is odd, don't you think?" Philippa said. She'd been pretty quiet up to now, but that's just Philippa. Always listening carefully for something she can use in one of her novels.

"How's that?" Richard asked.

"It all feels like it's a part of a whole, don't you think? I mean, first you have that odd rumor about Myrtle, then it was Edna's turn. Next was the rumor about Lillian. And now we have one that's aimed at Devi and Mac. Only the one about Edna was true. The one about Myrtle was both untrue and unkind, but these last two have been vicious."

"And what they all have in common is they've happened to friends of mine," I said. "So, do you believe me now?" I asked Norman, who'd dismissed my theory it was Susannah trying to hurt me through my friends.

"Did you ever get the envelope tested?" Devi asked.

"I sent it and the napkin off last week."

"Envelope? Napkin?" Norman said.

"Yes. The envelope the card sent to Myrtle came in, and a napkin Susannah used."

"And how did you collect this napkin?" Norman said, looking very stern.

"Lill helped me. After all, she and I were partners in crime-solving long before you and I met."

"So you expect this will be proof of what?" Norman asked.

"If the DNA on the envelope matches Susannah's, it proves she's connected to the rumor about Myrtle and, in my opinion, that's strong circumstantial evidence that she's behind the others as well."

"I get it that maybe you two didn't have the warmest relationship, but what I don't get is why, five minutes after she moves here, she would start waging a campaign against you," Norman said. "And an indirect one at that. One where she has no way of even knowing it bothers you, because wouldn't that be the point?"

"You're right. When you put it like that, it does seem unlikely. But what other explanation is there?"

"Well, if it is Susannah and she's going after all your friends, why haven't we been hit?" Philippa said. "I'm feeling a bit left out."

"Maybe she did her homework and found out

you used to be a lawyer," I told Philippa.

"But if you're right about her, she didn't hesitate to attack a police chief."

"Mac said whoever it was had pretty good computer skills," Devi said. "So maybe your turn is still coming. It has to take some thought and planning to carry all of this off."

"There is one other odd thing about it," Lill said. "Josephine and I have checked, and nobody remembers Susannah telling them the rumors, and nobody saw the notice about Edna being posted on the bulletin board. Given Susannah's so memorable, you'd think if she was the source, someone would've remembered her."

"I can think of only one way she could've pulled it off," I said. I'd been mulling over that question since the first rumor, and now, with an almost audible *click*, I knew there was a way, and it's probably what I'd do if I were trying to get a rumor off the ground anonymously.

"Through one of the staff," Lill said.

We smiled at each other.

"I agree. How about this?" I said. "A housekeeper arrives at Susannah's apartment and Susannah pretends to be on the phone, telling someone a juicy bit of gossip she's just heard. The housekeeper mentions it to other staff and, eventually, a resident hears it. It takes off from there."

"It's plausible," Philippa said. "Maybe she

tried that along with the note on the bulletin board and realized the rumor sharing worked better than the notice. Then, once she decided that passing a rumor through the staff was the way to go, she concocted that doozy about Lillian."

"If my checking proves she's the source of the rumors, and I don't have a single doubt about that, I think we should consider including her in the con." I was really feeling vengeful by that point. How dare Susannah hurt my friends?

"I want to keep the focus on Culpepper," Richard said.

"But if you can manage some collateral damage, why not go for it?" I said.

"Jo," Norman said.

"Just saying. She deserves to experience some sort of consequence. I'm not suggesting you take all her money, or even very much. Just give her a scare, maybe."

"Con?" Devi said.

I think we'd all forgotten her presence. Or I should say the implications of having the wife of the chief of police in our midst while we were planning a not completely legal operation.

"Better if you don't know the details," Richard said.

She gave each of us a look and then shook her

head. "Thanks for the help with the posts. I owe you."

"Not at all," Richard said. "We can't have citizens doubting Mac. Not good for the community."

"Speaking of Mac, that post about him was a completely different approach from the Brookside rumors," Norman said, giving Lill and me a look.

"Well, it's not unheard of for someone Susannah's age to be computer savvy. Does Mac have any ideas about how that was done?" I asked Devi.

"With a burner phone, I'll bet," Richard said. "Use it for this and then discard the phone. If she did that, there's no way to trace it. She might have even worn some kind of disguise and used cash when she bought the phone just in case the police department decided to get serious about tracing the post."

"It just hit me," said Philippa. "Didn't you say that Susannah usually eats with Myrtle, and isn't it almost time for dinner?"

"Oh, oh," Lill said.

"What?" I asked.

"What do you want to bet Myrtle will be eager to share all the excitements of her day with her new best friend, Susannah? I mean, why wouldn't she?"

"Already calling," Richard said.

We waited while the phone in Myrtle's apartment rang and rang.

Philippa looked at her watch. "Bet she's already on her way to dinner."

"I can try to head her off," Lill said. "You drive me back now, and I might even beat her to the dining room."

"Worth a try," Richard said.

"I'll take you," Devi said. "I need to get back. I left Maddie watching the twins."

Chapter Seventeen

Lillian

The dining room is only a few steps from the front door where Devi dropped me. I moved quickly to the entrance then stopped to look for Myrtle, fingers crossed she wasn't there yet. Unfortunately, she and Susannah were just sitting down at their usual table.

Since I'm not one to give up before everything plays out, I marched over to them. "I hope you don't mind me joining you?"

I didn't wait for a response, simply pulled out

a chair and sat. A signature Myrtle move.

Susannah gave me an insincere smile and said, "Of course not."

She and Myrtle were across from each other, so I was sitting between them.

"Lillian, I'm so glad you're here," Myrtle said. "You can help me tell Susannah all about what we did today."

So maybe I shouldn't have joined them? But no, I'm quite certain Myrtle was itching to tell the story with or without me. I felt under the table for Myrtle's foot and gave it a sharp tap. When she looked at me, I shook my head. Her mouth opened, but I couldn't let her speak.

"Yes. We went to Aglamesis for ice cream," I said, keeping up the pressure on Myrtle's foot. She moved it and gave me an annoyed look.

"To celebrate," she said, glaring at me.

Susannah looked up from her menu card. "Oh? What were you celebrating?" she asked.

"Myrtle got her quarterly statement from her financial advisor and it had really good news," I said, reaching out to tap Myrtle's foot yet again.

"I wish you'd stop kicking me," Myrtle said. "Really, Lillian."

"Sorry," I said. "I thought that was the table. Restless leg syndrome, don't you know."

"I doubt you thought any such thing. You're just trying to shut me up. I know you. But I don't see any reason not to share our little adventure with Susannah. You know she won't say anything."

I didn't know any such thing, but I couldn't think of what else I could do to shut Myrtle up, short of grabbing her scarf and gagging her with it. Thank goodness we weren't sitting anywhere near the Culpeppers and Winstons, who were once again sitting together, and I say so much for Roxanne Culpepper despising the Winstons.

My only options to distract Myrtle from her bone were to fake either choking or a heart attack, but since no food had been delivered, choking was out, and a heart attack would only delay the inevitable, and besides, I'd miss dinner.

But maybe I could confuse things a bit.

"Myrtle," I said, in my sternest, if-you-don't-behave-there-will-be-dire-consequences voice perfected during my years of teaching. "You know good and well we're not supposed to tell anyone about that fund. After all, Josephine swore us all to secrecy. Do you want to take a chance on it all going away?"

I know this statement didn't make much sense. But I hoped it would remind Myrtle she shouldn't talk about an ongoing operation. To anyone.

"Well, I just know Josephine won't mind me telling Susannah. They're friends from way back, you know."

Of course they're not! I eyed the scarf Myrtle was wearing with longing. Even better, a piece of duct tape would not go amiss.

"I have a better idea. Why not have Susannah talk to Josephine herself. If Josephine wants to share the information, it will be her choice, not ours." I turned toward Susannah. "Josephine is an incredibly successful investor." Then, remembering how Myrtle had handled Roxanne, I continued. "I expect you know all about the Edward Hopper painting she owns. Hopper's paintings now sell for millions, and that painting only scratches the surface of Josephine's assets."

"Oh, I had no idea," Susannah said.

"Yes, Lillian's absolutely correct," Myrtle said. "You should talk to Josephine."

I moved my foot away from Myrtle's and picked up my menu card, sighing with relief. I had no idea if I'd managed to keep the plan in place or not. But for sure, after dinner, I'd have to talk to Myrtle privately and urge her not to say anything more to Susannah, and then I'd let Josephine know what a close call we'd had.

Happily, the rest of the dinner conversation was about Susannah's cat that, according to her, was as smart as a monkey. I still couldn't wrap my head around the idea of Susannah as an animal lover. Is it possible to love animals and be cruel to humans? I suppose it must be, because the opposite is clearly true.

By the time dinner ended, I thought the danger was over. But when I offered to walk with Myrtle back to her apartment just to be sure, Susannah butted right in and said she and Myrtle planned to attend the concert being given that evening.

"Lovely. I'd forgotten there was a concert," I said, although we seemed to have one every few days with Christmas so close. "Why don't I come with you?" I was determined to stay by Myrtle's side until I got a chance to speak with her privately.

"Terrific," Susannah said, in a tone that suggested it was anything but.

"Oh, I'm so glad you're joining us, Lillian," Myrtle said. "We don't seem to see that much of each other anymore. And I do love Christmas music."

On the way to the concert, I even followed Myrtle to the bathroom. But so did Susannah. It was almost as if Susannah was on a mission to make sure I wasn't left alone with Myrtle, although that made no sense.

I did lag behind the two coming out of the bathroom so I could give Josephine a quick call to alert her to the situation. And may I just say that I'm so glad Josephine insisted on me getting a cell phone. I don't use it often, but when I need it, I really, really need it.

"You need reinforcements," Josephine said when I told her what was happening.

"Why don't you send Norman," I said. "He can sit next to Susannah and talk to her while I get in a few words with Myrtle. Or we can do the opposite. I can talk to Susannah while he whispers in Myrtle's ear."

"Let me check," she said.

After a minute, she was back on the line. "He's on his way. He said he'll play it by ear when he gets there."

I ended the call feeling relieved that some of the responsibility for saving the scheme had been lifted from my shoulders. I hurried to catch up with Myrtle and Susannah, urging them to take seats where Norman would have a spot next to Susannah. Although I'd offered it as a suggestion, I really didn't want to be the one to distract her. I don't have much of a poker face, except when I'm playing poker.

Norman arrived only a couple of minutes behind us—Myrtle is a very slow walker, thank goodness—and sat next to Susannah.

"Norman Neuman," Myrtle said. "And where is that lovely wife of yours?"

"Wrapping Christmas presents," Norman said.

"Oh, my goodness. She's so organized. I've barely started shopping."

As the exchange of small talk continued, I could see I wasn't going to get a word in edgewise with Myrtle. Even though Norman was sitting one seat over, with Susannah in between, Myrtle leaned forward and continued to monopolize him. And she didn't sit back until the concert started. I waited for a short break between songs, then leaned over and tapped Myrtle's arm. I spoke directly into her ear. Not loudly, you understand, because I didn't want her hearing aid to object.

"You mustn't say anything more to Susannah or anyone else about our little caper," I said.

"Why not?" Myrtle whispered back. Another song was being introduced, so I spoke quickly.

"You have to keep it secret until Richard tells you it's okay to say something."

"Oh, all right. If you insist." She settled back in her seat, her bracelets *ka-ching*ing, and I breathed a sigh of relief at the thought I could stop turning myself into a pretzel trying to get through to Myrtle. Instead, I could relax and enjoy the concert.

Chapter Eighteen

Devi

A few days before Christmas, Mac called me at work. It was something he never did unless there was an emergency. My first thought was that it had something to do with the social media post, but it had been mostly taken care of, although we were still dealing with the bad taste of the aftermath. Norman, Richard, and Maddie's posts, along with an explanatory post from the city manager, and possibly the proximity of Christmas, had let the air out of the most fervent anti-posters.

Unfortunately, the city manager had followed up by meeting with Mac and telling him it might be a good idea for us not to do any more house-sitting. That was upsetting, but luckily, we'd already begun planning to look for a place of our own. I just preferred it to be on our schedule, not an arbitrary one based on poorly informed and irate citizens. I sighed at the thought, brought back to the present moment by Mac's "Devi?"

"What is it, love?" I asked.

"It's Lisa."

Of course it was.

"She's been taken to the hospital. Can you possibly come and take care of Mika while I get it sorted out?"

"Where are you?"

"At Lisa's apartment."

Maddie and I commute together, and we take turns driving. Since it had been my turn that morning, I told Mac I'd be able to come right away.

When I arrived at Lisa's apartment, I found Mac's police car in front and him inside, pacing, with Mika in his arms.

He kissed me in welcome and Mika waved a tiny hand as if also greeting me.

"Thanks for getting here so quickly."

"So, you'll be willing to see if you can get a speeding ticket voided?" At the look on his face, I caved. "No ticket. Light traffic. What's going on with Lisa?"

"She showed up at a neighbors' door this morning in her nightgown, jabbering a mile a minute. They thought she was on drugs and called 911. One of the officers who responded recognized her and called me instead of social services, thank goodness."

"You said they took her to the hospital?"

"Yeah. I really don't think it's drugs," Mac said. "I took a look around, and I didn't see any signs."

"If not drugs, then what?"

"She's always had a problem with depression, but this is something different."

I thought back to all the interactions I'd had with Lisa. For sure, there had been times after the twins were born when I'd wondered about her mental state.

"So, what do you need me to do?"

"Is it okay with you if we take Mika home with us? Whatever's going on with Lisa, she's not going to be able to take care of her for at least a few days."

His request took me back to the twins' birth. Lisa had hit a wall emotionally soon after, and Mac and I had to step in to care for Lily and Toby, an arrangement that had evolved into a permanent one.

"Of course, we'll take her," I said.

He closed his eyes, and I could see he was relieved. Although there really was no other response either of us could make.

"Love you, Devi McElroy."

"Of course you do," I said, standing on my toes so I could kiss him. "Because I'm totally awesome."

"You are." He kissed me back, then handed me Mika, along with her bottle.

"I'll call as soon as I know anything."

"We'll see you at home, then," I said.

I finished feeding Mika, and then I organized her clothing, diapers, and equipment and carried it all down to the car. That was when I realized I didn't have an infant car seat. But Lisa had to have one. I looked around and found car keys in the kitchen. Then I stood on the balcony, clicking the keys until I spotted her car. I got the infant seat transferred and went upstairs one last time to collect Mika.

As I was closing Lisa's door, the door across the way opened and an elderly woman stuck her head out.

"Is she going to be okay?" she asked.

I wasn't sure whether she was asking about Lisa or the baby. But the answer was the same for both. "I'm sure she is."

"I was so worried this morning. She had to be freezing. Barefoot and everything."

Barefoot? That couldn't be good, since Lisa's apartment opened to an outside stairwell.

"Are you with social services?" the woman said, snapping my attention back to her.

"No, I'm Lisa's friend." For sure, I didn't want to get into the whole Lisa-is-my-husband's-ex-wife explanation.

"I saw the police were here."

"Yes, that's who called me. Thank you for

helping Lisa this morning."

"Well, that's what we're supposed to do, isn't it?"

"It is. Still, as her friend, I want you to know how much I appreciate it."

I'd been disturbed before I got here, but this report raised my concerns about Lisa to a new level. I thought for a moment the neighbor and I were at a stand-off, but then the woman shivered.

"Well, it's cold out here. I better let you get that baby into a warm car." And with that, she pulled her door shut. I was left holding Mika and wondering what the future would bring.

Chapter Nineteen

Josephine

In the midst of the final countdown to Christmas, I took a break from wrapping paper, tape, and bows and went over to the main building to meet with Lill and her housekeeper.

"Do you know who cleans Susannah Rasmussen's apartment?" Lill asked the woman.

"What apartment's she in?"

"Number Ten, Snap-Tit," Lill said.

"Ooh, we always stick the new girl with that wing."

"Because of the name?" I asked.

"Well, sure, that'd be one reason. But mainly 'cause it seems to attract residents who ain't so nice."

"But surely, it's a random thing," I said. "There have to be nice and not-so-nice people scattered everywhere in the complex."

"There are. Just seems like more of them not-so-nice ones end up in Snap-Tit. Except for Mrs. Grabinowitz. She's a sweetheart. Apartment's a bear to clean, though."

"Poetic justice," Lill said, referring, I expect, to the fact that not-nice people deserved to have the least desirable Brookside address.

"So who's the new girl?"

"She ain't so new no more. But she's still bottom of the pecking order. Name's Shania, and I think I need to warn youse. She's a turrible gossip and a snoop. So don't say nothing in front of her you don't want the world to hear about. She's the one told me about you," she said, glancing at Lill. "Course I didn't believe a word, but that story were like a wildfire. Now I think on it, 'spect it were Shania done a lot of the spreading."

"Just so you know," I said, "there wasn't a

speck of truth in that rumor."

"Didn't think there was. Glad to know I was right."

We thanked her and left her to her duties while we went in search of Shania. We found her supplies and equipment parked outside Darlene's door. We looked at each other, and as frequently happened, came to the same conclusion simultaneously.

"Why don't we leave her a note?" Lill said.

"Good idea." Even if Lill wasn't feeling it, I was uncomfortable hanging out so close to the Winstons' apartment. And who knew when Shania might emerge. I pulled out one of the index cards I carry with me. I was about to hand it to Lill, when it hit me that if Shania was the source of the rumors, she would likely recognize Lill's name and maybe hesitate to get in touch. After thinking about if for a moment, I wrote the note instead, asking Shania to call me when she had a chance—that I needed to ask her a question. As I added my phone number, it did occur to me that asking about the rumors might be tricky. I'd have to give my approach some thought before I spoke to her.

Lill looked over what I'd written and nodded in agreement. I found a place to prop the note where Shania should notice it and then, moving briskly, we got out of Snap-Tit. There really did seem to be a dark vibe. Not that I'm into vibes.

And neither is Lill, but if anything, I had to pick up my pace to keep up with her.

"Whew," she said as we reached one of the seating areas at a junction between wings. It had the mandatory glass case of birds and a scattering of flowering orchids—all part of the birds and flowers theme that permeates the complex. One nice perk is that once the orchids finish blooming, they're replaced, and the plants go to anyone who wants one. Lill has rescued several and has a wonderful knack for getting them to bloom again.

Without discussing it, we sat down and gave each other a relieved look.

"It does have a dark feel," I said. "Or maybe we're just victims of suggestion."

"Hmph. I'm just feeling relieved to get out without running into one of those not-nice people," Lill said.

"So now we wait to hear from Shania," I said, thinking it would probably not be until the end of her shift. At that moment, my phone rang. I pulled it out and glanced at the number. Shania already, and I hadn't had a chance to think about what I'd say.

After a brief hesitation, I answered. She greeted me, sounding curious.

"Oh, yes. Shania. Thank you for calling me

back so quickly." I put the phone on speaker so Lill could hear.

"Do I know you?"

"I don't believe so. But I'm a resident, and someone told me you have a finger on the pulse here and know almost everything that goes on. They said you're the best one to answer a question I have."

"Oh, I do know a lot," she said.

So flattery was still an effective way to distract a person from a very peculiar interaction. Thank goodness.

"I have a dreadfully curious nature," I said. "It will be the death of me yet, I expect."

"Oh, I doubt that," Shania said.

"Well, here's what I'm curious about. It's some of the recent goings on here at Brookside. I'm hoping you can help me."

"I'd be happy to try."

"Wonderful. What I'm wondering about is that weird story that went around recently about Myrtle Grabinowitz. Did you hear it?"

"Indeed I did. I felt so bad for her. Mrs. Grabinowitz is a lovely lady, and I just hated to think that something so horrible happened to her."

"Do you remember where you first heard the story? I mean, did Mrs. Grabinowitz tell you about it?"

"Oh, no. Of course not. No, no. I heard it from . . . let me think, was that a Tuesday or a Wednesday?"

I waited without speaking for her to work through it.

"You know, I believe I heard it from Mrs. Brady."

Not Susannah. That was a disappointment.

"But I'm not quite sure," Shania continued. "Now if you're wondering about rumors, there was a real doozy going around about that Mrs. Fitzel, and I can tell you exactly where I heard that one."

"Oh, yes. That would be good."

"It was that new resident. That Mrs. Rasmussen. Well, she was talking to Mrs. Brady. Or maybe that was when I heard the rumor about Mrs. Grabinowitz."

"You heard Mrs. Rasmussen tell someone that Mrs. Fitzel's husband was a drug dealer? Is that what you're saying?" I knew I was leading the witness, but this wasn't court after all, and the longer we talked, the more confused Shania seemed to be.

"No. No, I'm wrong. I know exactly what happened. I was dusting in the bedroom, and I heard Mrs. Rasmussen on the phone, telling that story about Mrs. Fitzel to someone. I don't know who. It sure shook me up, I can tell you that."

"So you don't know who she was talking to?"

"Nope. I don't believe she said a name."

"So afterward, did you mention it to anyone? After all, it was certainly a startling bit of information."

"Oh, yes. I told several of the staff. I mean, we all need to know what we're dealing with, don't we?"

"Do you have any idea how residents might have come to hear about it?" I asked.

"Well, maybe from Mrs. Rasmussen. Or maybe one of the staff. We do chat with people while we clean. Least I do."

That comment reaffirmed my decision to be elsewhere when our cleaner comes.

"Well, I can assure you there isn't a speck of truth in that rumor," I said.

"There isn't? You mean Mrs. Rasmussen was lying? On purpose? Well, that's a mean thing to do."

"I don't know if it was on purpose. But here's the thing. I know Mrs. Fitzel very well. She and her husband were both schoolteachers. So if you hear anyone saying different, you can let them know they're wrong."

"Well, I'll certainly do that. It's wicked of someone to tell a lie like that."

"Yes, it is. So, do you happen to remember

when you heard about Mrs. Grabinowitz?" I thought it was worth another shot.

"You know, that was a while back. But seems like it was something similar. Mrs. Rasmussen talking to somebody on the phone, or maybe having a cup of tea with someone. Just don't persactly remember."

"Well, thank you so much for your help. I really, really appreciate it." It appeared we had our answer, or as close as we were likely to get. It wouldn't stand up in court, of course, but it satisfied me that I was right about Susannah.

I clicked the phone off and looked at Lill. "Two birds, one stone, you think?" Meaning, first, we'd gotten the information we needed and, second, just maybe, we'd also countered the lie about Lill.

"One can only hope she's as good at passing around the truth as she is a lie," Lill said.

There was only one other small piece of the puzzle still pending, the DNA test. I'd sent it off, but hadn't yet received a report. But it no longer mattered because Shania had just confirmed I was correct in thinking Susannah was the guilty party.

That meant our next step was to serve up some consequences. And really, isn't that exactly the sort of thing everyone wants to be doing this close to Christmas?

Chapter Twenty

Devi

By the time I got home with Mika and got her settled, it wasn't worth it for me to go back to work. I called Maddie to let her know what had happened. She said not to worry, that Oliver would bring her home.

Annie, happy for the chance to make a bit extra before Christmas, immediately agreed to help with Mika. It would be for only a few days, since I was taking the week off between Christmas and New Year's, and surely, by New Year's things should be resolved.

When Mac got home, the first thing he did was call Nick, who would just be starting his day in Japan. I listened to Mac's side of the call as I prepared the twins' dinner. Mac, being both a cop and a man, quickly summarized what had been happening since Lisa's return to Cincinnati. Nick must have asked whether he needed to come home, and Mac's answer included the words, "first available flight." He ended the call and shook his head at me.

"Poor guy. Didn't have a clue what was going

on. Apparently Lisa hasn't called him in days and when they do talk she basically says she's fine, and when he asks when she's planning to come back to Japan, she always says, 'Soon.'"

"So, he's coming, right?"

"Flights are always pretty full before the holidays, but he'll come as soon as he can."

"And what about Lisa? Do you know how she's doing?"

"All I know is, she can only have family visitors for at least forty-eight hours."

"That sounds ominous."

"I think it's more that it's their protocol for patients as agitated as Lisa apparently was."

"You can't say it's a police matter and insist on an update?"

"HIPAA privacy rules, love. It's likely we'll find out she's been discharged when she shows up here. But Nick will be here soon, and he can take over."

From your lips to God's ears, I thought. But I didn't say it. One thing Mac and I both try to do is to keep a positive attitude about Lisa.

As for Nick, he couldn't arrive soon enough.

Chapter Twenty-One

Josephine

"Exactly how legal is what we're planning to do?" I asked Richard at our next huddle. After having some time to think about it, I was feeling a slight niggle of concern.

"In the strictest sense, questionable, I suppose," Richard said. "But after all, we're simply trying to recover what the mark stole from our client. Bottom line, setting legalities aside, I'd say there's nothing unethical about it."

"So, are we letting Mac know what's going on?" I asked. It was one thing to con a murderer to confess using enhanced adult beverages. It was a whole other thing to do something wonky involving money and possibly wire transfers.

"I think he'd prefer us to carry on."

I considered that code for, "No, we're not telling him because he'd stop us."

"You're not getting cold feet, are you?" Lill said. "Seems to me, you steal from someone, they're within their rights to take it back."

"We need to be careful, though."

"Of course we do," Richard said.

I glanced at Norman, who was watching me with an amused twist to his lips.

"Don't think I don't notice you aren't saying anything, Mr. Neuman."

He scratched his neck and smiled. "It's not like you to worry about legal niceties in a situation like this, Jo. Besides, I think you can count on your relationships with several of the FBI's finest, as well as Mac, to have your back."

"And funnily enough, what I can visualize is myself on a work detail picking up trash along the highway."

"Doubt that," Richard said. "After all, look at the cushy job Edna got. Reading to kiddies, wasn't it?"

"So that job's taken," I said, just to be contrary.

"I thought she'd completed her community service," Philippa said.

"She did," Lill said. "But she liked it so much, she's still doing it."

"Trust me, I would not ask for an extension on a trash pickup sentence," I said.

"Oh, I don't think you'd be on trash pickup, Josephine," Lill said. "This is probably much more serious than that. They might have to lock you up." She tried, unsuccessfully, to smother a chuckle.

"You're not helping," I told her.

"You're not even the one at risk here," Norman said. "It's mostly on Richard. All we'll be is accessories."

"Now you're all just being silly," I said. "I do think it's legitimate to worry about consequences."

"Agreed," Richard said, throwing up his hands. "No wire transfers, okay?"

"So what will you do instead? I mean you're talking a lot of money."

"It may be old fashioned, but a personal check still works just fine. But first, we may have to do something else to finish roping Culpepper in."

"How about we don't even think about that until after Christmas," I said.

"Works for me," Richard said.

Except, there was one thing I needed to do, and despite being the one to suggest we wait until after Christmas, I wanted to get it out of the way as soon as possible.

~ ~ ~

I called the Frosties to tell them that my investigation into the investment Charlie Culpepper had suggested for them was complete, and that I had sufficient concerns that I'd told

Lill to take a pass. And I hoped they would as well.

"Investments like the one he's proposing make the most sense for younger investors."

"It sounds good, though," one of them said. "I like the idea of guaranteed income for life."

"Consider this, though. You'll never be able to touch the principal, and if you should die in less than twenty-five months, the balance of the investment won't go to your heirs; it will revert to the fund manager."

"In other words, you're saying the downside outweighs the positive of the monthly payout." I suspected that was Martha speaking.

Of course the main reason I knew without a doubt this investment was a terrible idea was because Charlie and Roxanne would be leaving Brookside soon, one way or the other, and if Mary and Martha invested now, their money would be socked away in the Caymans and untraceable.

"Do you need the monthly payout?" I asked.

"It might be nice to have a bit more, but we don't actually need a thousand."

"It just sounded good."

"In that case you're better off leaving your money in savings and withdrawing what you need when you need it."

"I suppose."

"So, you won't give any money to Charlie to manage, right?"

"Well, he sure wasn't happy when we said we wanted to delay. He'll probably be really annoyed with us if we don't go ahead."

"We can just tell him we weren't able to pull together the twenty-five thousand," one of the voices said.

It really is quite dizzying carrying on a phone conversation with the two of them.

"Oh, yes. We can say we spent more for Christmas than we anticipated." I was pretty sure that was Mary, inasmuch as I'd been able to separate the two.

"I know. Let's just tell Roxanne, and she can tell him."

It sounded to me like this was a discussion that could take some time.

"You'll let me know how it goes," I said.

"Oh, yes" and "Indeed we will" overlapped.

I ended the call with a sigh of relief, my duty done.

~ ~ ~

Roxanne Culpepper called the next day, and my immediate thought was it must have something to do with the Frosties pulling out of the investment.

"I've heard so many interesting things about you, Josephine. And I feel like we have so much in common." She paused. I remained silent, reordering my thoughts.

"Yes. Well, I'd really, really like to meet you and get to know you. And I know this is a busy, busy time, right before Christmas, but sometimes things get really quiet after Christmas, and I thought perhaps a girls' night out, or really, in, would appeal. I thought I'd invite a couple of other residents. Not too many, you know. Just three or four, so we can have a really nice visit. Like a Tupperware party, but without the Tupperware."

I opened my mouth to say I was planning a visit to Timbuktu and wouldn't be available when it hit me. We'd expected the Culpeppers to contact Richard after they read the bogus financial report. But maybe after what Myrtle told them about me, they'd changed tactics. Maybe they were now interested in scamming me out of some of the millions Myrtle had credited me with. Whichever it was, it appeared the ball was clearly in my court.

"That sounds like fun. I always feel a bit letdown after Christmas," I said, trying to temper my tone to sound engaged but not too eager.

"Lovely. Are you available the Thursday

after?"

"Yes, that would work for me. Who else are you inviting?"

"I was thinking Chantelle Winston and maybe Myrtle Grabinowitz."

"Oh, I'm not sure that's such a good idea," I said. "You may recall that recently Myrtle had some not very nice things to say about Chantelle's husband."

Roxanne tittered. "That's exactly why I'm inviting them. Just because our men do something we disapprove of doesn't mean we women need to hold a grudge. Besides, I've already talked to Chantelle, and she's fine with Myrtle being there."

Then far be it from me to object. I wished I had more time to think about what my strategy should be. But there was one way to gain some time.

"May I bring a guest?" I said.

"Oh, well, I suppose that would be okay. Not your husband, though."

Definitely not. "He's not much of a fan of girls' nights." I grimaced at the fake cheery tone I'd adopted. But I needed to sound somewhat enthusiastic if I was going to be able to fool them.

"Well, okay," Roxanne said. "We're set then. I'll see you and your guest Thursday at seven."

That left me with the dilemma of whom, if anyone, to invite. Philippa was a possibility, but Lill was my first choice. Although, perhaps not in this particular situation, since Chantelle was going to be there. On the other hand, Lill's inclusion would possibly unsettle Chantelle, and that might be rather interesting to observe.

Another plus would be that Lill is fully briefed on the plan to scam the Culpeppers and thus would be an asset I could count on no matter what direction the evening took.

Lill. Of course it had to be Lill.

Chapter Twenty-Two

Devi

Nick arrived two days before Christmas. Although Mac invited him to stay with us, he'd declined, saying he'd just stay in the apartment Lisa had been renting, but that he'd stop by to pick up the key, if that was all right with us.

We didn't hear from him for several hours after his flight landed. We were just clearing from dinner when he showed up. He'd been to the hospital, he said. He looked tired and strained, but that could have been because of the long flight. He asked to see Mika first thing. I considered that a good sign.

Since she was due to be fed, I warmed a bottle and gave it to him, and Mac steered him to the room we use as our family room. Mac gave me a look that I interpreted to mean he'd talk to Nick while I put the twins to bed. I nodded with relief. I didn't think it was going to be an easy conversation, so better if Mac handled it. The twins fussed a bit because Mac didn't come to kiss them goodnight, but I read them an extra story, and by the time it ended, they were both asleep.

I went downstairs, and as I passed the family room, Mac called to me to join them.

"Do you want me to put her down?" I asked. I could see Mika had finished her bottle and was asleep in Nick's arms.

"Guess you better. I sit here with her much longer, I'm liable to fall asleep too."

"I see Mac has been seducing you with Scotch," I said, taking Mika from him. "I think you'd better plan to spend the night."

"I suppose you're right," he said. "I'm about wiped out. Probably shouldn't drive."

"You absolutely shouldn't," I said. "You get in your car, Mac will just have to arrest you. We have plenty of room. Have you eaten?"

"Yeah. On the plane."

"Hours ago, then. You'd better have something. Is grilled cheese okay?"

"Thanks."

I put Mika in her improvised crib, got out clean sheets for Nick, and then came back downstairs and fixed him a sandwich.

Mac let me know with another of his looks that he wanted me to join them. Nick took a huge bite of the sandwich, and as he chewed, Mac told me some of what they'd been discussing—that Lisa had been increasingly depressed since Mika's birth and the only thing that perked her up was the possibility of coming back to the States for the holidays.

"Were you able to visit her?" I asked, deciding to cut to the chase.

Nick nodded, his mouth engaged with another bite. I was beginning to think I needed to make a second sandwich.

"The good news is they don't think she has schizophrenia, and it's probably not manic depression."

Wow. Manic depression had occurred to me, but schizophrenia hadn't.

"They suspect a severe case of postpartum depression exacerbated by a lack of sleep."

"Will she be in the hospital long?" I asked.

"At least another week, but likely two, so they can be sure she's sleeping okay and responding to the medication. It takes a couple of weeks for that to kick in."

"What then?" I asked.

He shook his head, then started to rub his forehead. "She absolutely hates it in Japan. But I can't leave her here on her own, responsible for taking care of a baby."

I was starting to feel uncomfortable about the answers we were getting. "Would you like another sandwich?" I asked, picking up his empty plate.

"No, no, I'm fine. I wouldn't mind making the acquaintance of that bed, though."

He went to get his suitcase out of his car, and I showed him upstairs. I came back down to find Mac in the kitchen, finishing the dinner cleanup.

"So?" I said.

"So he's got some very tough decisions to make."

"I'll say."

"One possibility he's considering is for Lisa and the baby to stay with his folks in Seattle until he comes back to the States."

"And does he have another? Possibility, that is?"

"Aside from insisting she return to Japan with him? Doesn't sound like it."

"You didn't offer for her to stay with us?"

"No. Because I think that's a truly dreadful idea."

Thank goodness, because so did I.

"He can't meet with his boss to discuss the situation until after Christmas. But for the moment, he's on compassionate leave."

"I guess we can hope that he won't have to go back to Japan. That maybe he can simply return to Cincinnati."

"Yeah, I'd say that would be the best thing."

Or even better, I thought, but didn't say it, if he were transferred somewhere else. In the States, but a long way from Cincinnati.

Because of the twins, we'll always have an unbreakable connection to Lisa, whether we want it or not, but it would be so much more bearable if that connection was at a distance.

"He also asked if Mika can continue to stay with us on the days he has meetings, and I told him that would be okay."

The only problem with that plan was that I was becoming quite attached to Mika, and with attachment came worry about her being raised by an unstable mother.

I shook my head sharply, trying to banish that thought. After all, Nick would be there, making sure Lisa and Mika were okay. And if Lisa did have postpartum depression, it should be treatable, and once she recovered, she should be fine. Would be fine.

As I dried the odds and ends Mac was washing, my thoughts drifted back to the holiday party we'd held such a short time ago. How excited I'd been to have all our friends over. How I'd felt like this was going to be a special Christmas.

Instead, what we were getting was an unusual Christmas. Not at all what I'd been dreaming of.

Chapter Twenty-Three

Myrtle

My goodness, what a struggle it's been, not to say something to Susannah about Richard's little plot. The RLP. That's what I'm calling it. I don't know what Richard calls it. The reason it's been so difficult not to slip up is this: Susannah keeps asking me about my investments and how I've managed to do so well. Honestly, for a while there I thought she was auditioning to be a woman detective on a crime show. Really, it was that bad.

I finally told her I didn't actually have a clue

about my investments. That my son handles all that for me. Without advice from Josephine, I might add. Although Josephine is really successful, so maybe I should have him ask her for suggestions.

So then Susannah said if my son was handling everything, why was I getting reports? And I had to think fast and say that my son always sends me something right before Christmas to let me know I still have plenty of money. That I suspect he does it so I'll be sure to buy him a nice present.

After that, I managed to get her to talk about her plans for Christmas. She said she was spending the day with her younger son. But she didn't sound happy about it. I thought that was odd. But I didn't take too much time thinking about that since it gave me an opening to talk about my family. There are such a lot of them, and most people just aren't interested, but Susannah usually acts as if she is. I'm not sure she was this time, though. She seemed very distracted.

I wonder if maybe she has money worries. I'm not sure why I think that. Oh, yes, I suppose because she keeps asking about my investments. Thank goodness I got that stopped. I really didn't want to say something that would mess up whatever it is that Richard has planned.

And Richard may not be the only plotter in

our midst. Today at lunch I saw Charlie Culpepper accost—a great crossword word—Mary and Martha as they came into lunch. The three stood speaking for a short time. Then Charlie turned and walked back to his table, and I could see what it means to say someone looks like thunder. My word, that man looked angry.

Mary gripped Martha's arm as they watched Charlie walk away, and the two of them looked shaken. I waved and caught their attention and motioned for them to join Susannah and me. They sat down, both of them breathing as if they'd just run a race.

"My goodness," I said. "You two look like a couple of ghosts." Their faces were as white as their hair, the part that isn't colored, I mean.

"And what's gotten up Charlie's craw?" I added, hoping to get them to share what it was all about.

"My goodness," Martha finally said, "I had no idea that man could be so unpleasant."

"But what was it about?" I asked.

"We just told him we've decided not to invest in a fund he told us about. You'd have thought we canceled Christmas."

"Charlie Culpepper runs an investment fund?" I said, trying to adjust my thinking about the man. He seems so unassuming, but he sure didn't look unassuming as he walked away from Mary and Martha a few minutes ago.

"Well, we're not exactly sure he runs it. Probably someone else does, and he just gets a commission when he talks someone into investing."

That was Martha speaking. In spite of her slightly weird sartorial—love my crosswords—choices, I think she's much sharper than Mary.

"To tell you the truth, it was Josephine who warned us about him," Mary said.

"Hush," Martha said. "That part is secret."

"Oh, we won't say a word. Will we, Susannah?"

"Not a word."

But for me, those two words, *Josephine* and *secret*, brought to mind the RLP. I still didn't know exactly what it was all about, but Richard did say he was checking on both the Culpeppers and the Winstons, which made Martha and Mary's interaction with Charlie Culpepper all the more mysterious and intriguing.

Chapter Twenty-Four

Josephine

Christmas Eve, the phone rang shortly after breakfast. The caller was a Brookside resident, but it wasn't a number I recognized. I debated about answering, but curiosity won out.

"Oh, Josephine, I'm so glad I caught you. I've wanted to talk to you for simply days."

The caller was Susannah. She hadn't identified herself, but I'd recognize that nasal twang anywhere.

"Of course I know you must be incredibly busy with Christmas, so I won't take up much of your time. But I just wanted to follow up on something Myrtle told me recently before I forget. She and I have become very good friends, you know."

"Myrtle is a very friendly person," I said, curious but not wanting to get sucked in.

"She is. And a very successful one, I've recently learned."

"Oh, yes. She has an amazing family. I have no idea how she managed all that," I said, being purposefully obtuse.

"Yes. Wow. Six children, wasn't it? I quite

agree, that's an amazing accomplishment."

"Five. Five children."

"And that isn't her only success," Susannah said. "The other day, she shared with me her amazing investment success."

Again, I refused to engage.

"Yes, well, anyway. She'd just gotten her quarterly report, and she was telling me about how one of the investments you suggested is doing fantastically well. And, well, she couldn't remember the exact details, so she said I should call you. So, here I am."

There were so many things I wanted to say here:

Really? You consider yourself Myrtle's friend, do you? Perhaps you might want to check Webster's definition of the word.

So, why did you start nasty rumors about her and Lill and Mac?

Why would you think I'd ever do anything to benefit you after all the things you've done to me and my friends?

I finally settled on, "I'm sorry, but I don't know what investment you're talking about. Myrtle and I have discussed several possibilities, but I don't follow her around checking to see what she's decided to do."

"Oh, of course you don't. But surely you can remember the fund you have that's doing better than Warren Buffet."

"Maybe," I said, still trying to decide what to do.

"So, in the spirit of Christmas and our very long friendship, I thought you might share a name with me."

"His name was Daniel," I said.

That was one effect Susannah always had on me. She made me think about Daniel, and the words just slipped out.

There was a beat of silence.

"Oh. You mean your friend from New York. I'm afraid I didn't handle that well, and I'm sorry. I envied you, actually, so I decided to tease you, but I never told your husband. And if you'd taken me seriously about the purse, I would have paid you for it."

I tried to decide if the words were sincere. I judged it unlikely.

"Good to know."

"So?"

I sighed, making sure she heard it. "I expect it must have been the JLR fund. At least that's the one I'm getting the best returns with."

"Does Charlie Culpepper have anything to do with it?"

"Why would you ask that?"

"Oh, just something I heard at lunch yesterday. You know those two women with the colored hair? Apparently they told Charlie they weren't investing in something he'd suggested, and boy was he angry. One of the women said you were involved somehow."

Oh, just fudge it. "Charlie has nothing to do with any of my investments."

"Good. I didn't like the way he acted. Anyway, thank you for the info, Josephine. I do need to improve my portfolio. I didn't get as much for the house as I was hoping, and I'd hate to have to ask my sons to chip in."

For a second, she sounded almost human. But then I reminded myself of how nasty she'd been at Devi and Mac's party and the rumors she'd started, and that eliminated any sliver of sympathy.

~ ~ ~

We'd planned to have Christmas dinner at our house, but the guest list expanded beyond our capacity with the additions of Glory, Nick back from Japan, Devi's parents joining us from Kansas, and Richard and Philippa's plans derailed by bad weather. Devi had quickly offered their house. Norman kept his role as chef with the rest of us either helping with the twins and Mika or chopping and stirring something at Norman's direction.

Norman and I had gone to Christmas Eve services, but Maddie, Oliver, and Lill went to church together Christmas morning, and the three of them arrived around noon, Maddie and Lill dressed to the nines. Lill was wearing one of her amazing church hats, and so was Maddie. Maddie isn't tall like Lill, so the hat made her look like a mischievous child playing dress-up. I fixed them sandwiches, trying to stay out of Norman's way and without leaving too much of a mess behind.

In the end, thirteen of us sat down to the feast Norman had prepared, with a little help from his friends. And, despite Nick's worry about Lisa and Glory's about her dying friend, we managed to be quite a jolly group, setting aside all worries and concerns for at least that one day.

~ ~ ~

When Lill and I arrived at the Culpeppers' three days later for the girls' night, Roxanne opened the door with a smile of welcome that faltered when she saw Lill standing beside me.

"Oh," she said, cocking her head and clearly struggling to keep a smile in place.

"Thank you for having me," Lill said,

extending a hand that Roxanne shook briefly.

"Umm. Yes, of course."

If I'd had any doubts whether the Culpeppers shared the racist views of the Winstons, they'd just been set to rest. My only consolation was that Lill had known to expect this and had still insisted on accompanying me.

"We've been partners in crime-solving far too long for me to cede the floor to Myrtle," Lill had said, when I explained about the gathering and who was going to be there. "Besides, it should be interesting. At my age, I make it a rule to never take a pass on something that might be interesting. Might not have too many *interestings* left."

"Even if it gets you kidnapped?" I said.

"One of the best things ever happened to me," she said, with a straight face. Then she laughed.

Still, I knew facing down Chantelle and Roxanne was not going to be pleasant, nor was it likely to turn out to be one of the best things to happen to Lill.

"Please, come in," Roxanne said.

I could swear she was gritting her teeth. As we entered the living room, I made it a point to watch for Chantelle's reaction when she saw Lill. It was, as expected, a scowl that she quickly covered with an insincere smile.

"Yes, Josephine and I have met," she said, ignoring Lill.

"Indeed we have," I said. "I thought you might be interested in getting to know the person you've been lobbying to get rid of." I simply couldn't resist taking a poke at her.

Lill pulled on the back of my blouse. I knew I shouldn't be saying those things, but seeing Chantelle sitting there with that superior and condescending look on her face. Well, luckily at that moment, the doorbell rang and Myrtle came puffing onto the scene.

For once, I wasn't even a smidge put out at the way Myrtle always manages to step, even with a walker, directly into the center of attention. Besides, I was pretty sure the reason Roxanne wanted her here had to do with that glowing financial report. And that was also the reason Chantelle was tolerating her presence. And mine. And Lill's.

We all sat, and Roxanne took drink orders— tea, coffee, or white wine—and passed around some mixed nuts. Myrtle took a handful of nuts, looking disappointed. Any gathering without mini quiches or cookies in the offing is not a success in Myrtle's opinion. But failing to meet Myrtle's culinary standards was likely the least of this gathering's hurdles.

"You don't happen to have any cookies, do

you?" Myrtle asked.

"Oh, no. Sorry. Charlie and I are trying to eat better. Watching our cholesterol, you know."

"Doesn't do a bit of good to watch it," Myrtle said. "Cholesterol doesn't give a fig. I gave that up years ago. Watching. And I'm still here. Besides, if I have to give up cookies, I'd rather be dead."

"My goodness," Chantelle said. "I don't think ignoring cholesterol makes it go away. Why would there be all these drugs if that was the case? And you can't possibly mean that about cookies."

"Sure I do," Myrtle said. "Without cookies, where's the fun? And without fun, who needs to live?"

Lill and I watched this performance without looking at each other because, with one glance, we would have both cracked up. Myrtle was definitely playing with Roxanne and Chantelle, and clearly, Chantelle had fallen for it.

"And if there are no cookies, we need something to liven things up," Myrtle said. "Luckily, I know just the thing."

She reached for her tote and began digging through the contents.

"Here we are." She plunked a deck of cards and a box of paperclips on the coffee table.

"Probably best if we sit at the dining table. Don't you agree, Josephine?"

"How are we going to play cards?" Chantelle said. "There are five of us."

"Not a problem. The game I have in mind works with any number." Myrtle winked at me, and I knew exactly what she was planning.

"Come, ladies. And bring the nuts, Roxanne, if you please."

Roxanne, looking miffed, picked up the nuts and her drink. Myrtle pushed her walker out of the way, nearly tripping Chantelle, and walked the few steps into the dining room without it. She plopped into a seat at the foot of the table.

"I know what you're doing," Roxanne said. "You're suggesting we play poker."

"How clever of you," Myrtle said. "Indeed, I am. But I must give credit where credit is due. Josephine's the one who invented this game."

"Oh, I think poker's been around a very, very long time," Chantelle said.

"Not this version. Well, sort of, I suppose," Myrtle said. "We call it naked poker."

"Don't you mean strip poker?" Chantelle glanced around the group. "And I for one have no interest in seeing everyone's underwear choices."

"Oh, our version is different from that," Myrtle said. "We call it naked poker, but there's no disrobing involved. So nobody needs to get their panties in a twist. Instead, the loser has to tell a personal story about herself. Something juicy. And completely true, of course."

"Hmph," Chantelle said. "And how can you possibly know if it's completely true?"

"We caught a murderer playing naked poker," Myrtle said with a smug look.

Lill and I exchanged a glance at that *we caught*. But for the moment, neither of us was going to contradict Myrtle. She was definitely on a roll. She shoved the box of paperclips over to Lill, who began parceling them out. Then she picked up the cards and shuffled.

"You in?" she asked, glancing between Chantelle and Roxanne.

"I just thought we'd have a nice conversation, get to know something about each other," Roxanne said, sounding a bit desperate.

"Well, let's see," Myrtle said. "I know what we can do. Instead of an overall winner, or rather loser, and only one story, we can take turns having the loser of each hand tell a story." Myrtle looked at me and raised an eyebrow in question.

I nodded, and we were off.

"Does anybody need a refresher on the rules?" Myrtle asked.

"Of course not," Roxanne said. "I may not

play much, but I remember perfectly."

"As do I," Chantelle said. "And this is it? We play for paperclips?"

"Paperclips to keep track and stories to pay off our debts," I said, getting a sour look in return.

Myrtle is quite an expert shuffler. I expect she could get a job at the local casino if she wanted one. Within moments, we were all looking at our first hands. I'm not usually lucky with cards and tonight bore that out. I got terrible cards, but for once that suited me just fine.

By the time the hand ended, I'd lost, as intended, the most paperclips.

"That means you get to tell the story, Josephine," Myrtle said, in her role as grand arbiter.

Chantelle smirked at me, and if there's one thing I hate with a passion, it's a smirk.

"That works for me," I said. I'll see your smirk and raise you a cocked eyebrow.

"Let me think for just a moment." They sat looking at me, while I decided. But it wasn't difficult. I'd come here with a specific goal, after all, to confirm in Roxanne's mind that I was a canny and successful investor and had made lots and lots of money. And the naked poker game had just made that goal more easily achievable.

I told the story of how I'd circumvented my first husband's control of our finances by scrimping and saving the allowance he'd given me and using the excess to invest. I also mentioned the Edward Hopper painting, as additional proof I was a financial whiz.

"I must say, it's so exciting to know we have such clever new neighbors," Roxanne said when I finished.

"Another hand?" Myrtle said.

"Oh, yes. Let's," Chantelle said. "You're right, this is fun."

For the second hand, I ran a bluff with Lill's help. I wanted to catch Roxanne, but it was Chantelle who ended the round as the loser of the most clips.

"Oh, dear," she said. "I don't think I have a juicy story. Not like Josephine." She gave me a weak smile that I ignored.

"Why don't you tell us how you met and married your husband," Myrtle said.

"Of course. That's an excellent idea. Well, let's see, where to begin?"

"At the beginning," Myrtle said, bless her heart.

"Okay. Well, let's see. I met Andrew in high school, but we didn't date or anything. He was older and very popular, and I wasn't. Then I got married to another man. I'll call him Jim. I guess I married him because he asked me. I mean, I don't think I ever loved him. Anyway, Jim wasn't very nice. I mean, well, he didn't like any of my family, and I didn't have that many friends, but he didn't like them either. And then one day, he got mad because I hadn't ironed his shirts the way he wanted, and he hit me." She stopped speaking abruptly and took a breath as if she'd just realized she'd drifted off the point.

"Sorry. You asked about Andrew, didn't you. So, Andrew . . . After high school, I didn't see him for over fifteen years. And then, one day I ran into him in a store. He didn't remember me, or not exactly." She stopped and rocked back and forth. "But the funny thing is he remembered my name. Said he'd always liked it. We got to talking and the next thing I knew, we were having coffee and still talking. And, well, it just . . . we just . . . after a few months, he asked me to marry him, and here we are, thirty-one years later."

She stopped, and it looked to me like she was thinking about what she'd said. But there was a huge gap in the story.

"What happened to Jim?" Myrtle said. "Were you still married to him when you ran into Andrew again?"

Chantelle pursed her lips and then nodded as if making a decision before looking at Myrtle. "Well, that's definitely another story, and I only owed one, isn't that right?"

After a moment, Myrtle nodded. "I suppose

that's fair. But I'm guessing you gave Jim the old heave-ho. Over a cliff, perhaps? Or maybe you ran him down with your car or pushed him in front of a bus."

Chantelle looked startled, but then firmed her lips, leaving us all to wonder which one of Myrtle's guesses was correct, because it was clear Myrtle had either hit the mark directly, or had come mighty close.

I examined Chantelle surreptitiously, remembering my initial impression that she was weak and that Andrew was domineering. But right now, seeing the look in her eyes as she reacted to Myrtle's comments, I decided I sure wouldn't want to be on her bad side. I also briefly considered the possibility that she, not her blustery husband, was actually in charge of the Winston household.

I glanced at Lill to see she was frowning at Chantelle, so possibly she had the same thoughts I had.

Myrtle lost the next hand and told her usual story about being sabotaged by Miss Congeniality in the Miss America contest roughly a hundred years ago. Both Roxanne and Chantelle acted disbelieving until Lill and I said the story was absolutely true. Of course, we actually have no way of knowing that for sure, but since the story never changes, we give Myrtle the benefit of the doubt.

It was getting late by then, but Lill proposed one last hand. Which she lost. On purpose, in my estimation. She then folded her hands and rested them on the table and began speaking in slow, measured tones.

"As a child, I was a real good student. Loved school. Did real well. And when I brought home a report card with a bunch of As, my momma always made sure I got a treat. When I was ten, that treat was a quarter to spend in the small convenience store a block from our house. My best friend and I went together. We knew it was going to take some high-level deciding before we spent that quarter, and we were only a little way into our deliberations when the owner came up to us, grabbed us by our collars, and dragged us to the front of the store.

"My friend was holding a package of Twinkies and I had a hair ribbon, and we'd been discussing which we were going to purchase. See, even though it was my quarter, I always shared with my friend. But that man, he grabbed the Twinkies and the ribbon, and he yelled at us. Called us the N word. Nobody had ever called me that before. Guess I was just lucky. I had my quarter in one hand, the ribbon in the other, and when that man grabbed the ribbon and shoved us toward the door, I dropped the quarter."

My heart was aching by the time Lill had

gotten only partway through her story. I could well imagine how helpless she must have felt. A skinny little girl up against a full-grown man, and although she hadn't labeled him as White, I knew he had to have been.

"He picked that quarter up, gave me a look of satisfaction, and said he guessed I was a thief two times over. Then he dropped it in his pocket. When I said it was my quarter, and I was going to buy something, not steal, he just laughed. Told me to go home and not come back. Two of the people watching all this were two White girls a little older than we were, and they really were shoplifting. We'd watched as one looked around and the other slipped something in her pocket. They made faces at us when they noticed we were watching them. 'Course we knew to never put anything in our pockets until we'd paid for it."

She paused, and I could tell from the expression on her face, she was still feeling the pain of that false accusation.

"Oh, my goodness, Lillian," Myrtle said. "That's simply dreadful. You're saying that man picked on you because you were Black and ignored the real thieves who were White? Well, that's just not right. Not right at all. Did your momma go and give him what for and get your quarter back?"

I knew Myrtle tended to be naive, but this

comment proved she didn't have a clue how the world worked.

"I think it's more likely none of you set foot in that store again," I said, reaching out to touch Lill's hand.

"It was too hard on my momma not to shop there. You see, we didn't have lots of stores to choose from. But my friend and I never went back."

"I'm so sorry you were treated that way," I said. "Ever. By anyone."

Lill nodded at me, then abruptly got up and left the table, heading toward the bathroom. Since all the apartment designs are similar, she knew not to open the coat closet door by mistake.

"Well, my goodness," Myrtle said. "What a dreadful, dreadful way to treat a little girl."

"Or an elderly woman," I said, without looking at either Chantelle or Roxanne, neither of whom had said a word in support of Lill. I wondered if Roxanne was one of those people who would feel the need to spray her bathroom with Lysol because Lill had used it.

I would have liked to have seen Roxanne forced to tell a story, but consoled myself with the thought that between Lill and me, we'd accomplished most of what we'd hoped to, oddly enough, with Myrtle's unwitting help.

"Maybe we could talk about something less

weighty," Roxanne said, picking up all the paper clips and putting them back in their box. "Like your good fortune, Myrtle."

Lill returned to her seat next to me. When I gave her a questioning look, she nodded slightly to let me know she was okay.

"Oh, my, yes. We could talk about that," Myrtle said, sounding relieved. "But it isn't me you need to talk to. It's Richard. He handled the investment. He used to be a financial advisor, you know."

"Really?" Roxanne said. "How interesting. But I thought, Josephine, you were the one who suggested the fund to Myrtle."

"Oh, Josephine did," Myrtle said. "She suggested, but Richard was the one who organized it all for me. Josephine, why don't you tell them all about it?" she said, turning toward me.

"Richard's mostly retired, but lucky for us, he still keeps his hand in," I said. "And Myrtle and I have both been the beneficiaries of that. He just seems to be one of those people with a magic touch when it comes to picking the right companies and funds to invest in."

"Like you do, Josephine," Myrtle said, beaming.

"Sounds like Richard is someone else we

ought to meet," Roxanne said.

"Well, that's easy enough," Myrtle said. "He and Philippa live right here. I could introduce you."

"Oh, good," Roxanne cooed.

And with that, the evening became even more of a success than it was already, and we had Myrtle to thank for all of it. Lill and I excused ourselves, and Myrtle followed us out the door.

"Did I do good, Josephine?" Myrtle asked as we headed down the hall.

"You did excellently."

"I sure don't like that Chantelle. Didn't like the way she kept looking at you, Lillian. Even if she was abused. Do you think she murdered her husband? I do. And I also think she's no nicer than that current husband of hers. And did you know that Roxanne's husband suggested some sort of questionable investment to Mary and Martha? But of course you know, because you're the one who warned them not to give him the money. At least that's what Mary told us, right after it happened," Myrtle said. "At lunch yesterday."

I still didn't understand quite how Myrtle pulled off always being in the thick of things, but it should no longer come as a surprise.

We reached Myrtle's door and said our goodnights, and then I walked with Lill back to her place.

We stopped outside her door as she pulled her key out.

"Are you okay, Lill? I mean, your story. It broke my heart, but I don't think either Roxanne or Chantelle was the least bit touched."

"Like water etching stone, is that what you're saying?" Lill said.

"That's a good way to put it."

"A change of heart, hmm umm. Can't ever force it. Only thing to do is sneak up on it. That's all I did. Snuck up on it. Don't expect it'll make a difference right away. Or maybe ever. They've been thinking their way a very long time. Indeed they have. But I said my piece. Best I could do, so don't you worry about me."

"I do though."

"I know you do. I thank the Father every day for your friendship."

I swallowed over a lump in my throat. I don't have Lill's strong faith, but if God is watching over me in the personal way Lill believes He is, one of His gifts to me is Lill's friendship.

Chapter Twenty-Five

Myrtle

The first day of this particular New Year, my eighty-eighth on the planet, I slept right past my alarm. That was probably due to my participation in a small, low-key New Year's Eve celebration at Josephine's and Norman's.

Instead of the sparkling cider in plastic cups that other residents used to mark the occasion, we had champagne served in elegant crystal flutes. And there were delicious snacks, something I can always count on at Josephine's. Unlike at Roxanne's.

Edna, Lillian, and I didn't stay all the way to midnight, though. Norman drove us back around ten. But after all, it was midnight somewhere. This morning, rather than rushing around to make it to the dining room before it closed, I took my time, eventually breakfasting on cookies and milk. Since the cookies contained egg, oatmeal, and raisins, and milk was also involved, I'm quite certain my doctor would approve.

I'd just finished eating when Josephine called, and I told her of course I could meet her in the library at two o'clock so she could brief me—finally—on the details of our recent caper. And I just have to say, it's about time, although meeting in the library is a bit odd, as were her other instructions. I'm supposed to take off my bracelets, turn up my hearing aids, and sit in a dark corner. It all sounded deliciously mysterious.

I arrived at the library a few minutes before two and took a seat in the corner by the Christmas tree. Next time I get roped into one of Josephine's schemes, you can bet your boots I'm going to insist on the full particulars *before* I agree to play the lead. So there, Josephine.

I was starting to feel restless—sitting in a dark corner in a deserted room quickly loses its appeal—when Susannah entered the room. I opened my mouth to greet her, but when I saw Josephine was with her, I snapped it shut and sat very still.

Josephine ushered Susannah to a seat with her back to me while Josephine sat partially facing me, but not looking at me.

"So, what's this about?" Susannah asked.

"I want you to know that I know what you did, and if you do it again, I'll report you to the resident board." Josephine spoke slowly and distinctly, I assume for my benefit. I leaned toward them, straining to hear every word.

"I have no idea what you're talking about," Susannah said, sounding huffy.

And neither did I. What did Susannah have to do with Richard's Little Plot?

"You've been starting ugly rumors about my friends."

Oh, my. So, this wasn't about Richard at all.

"I still have no idea what you're talking about," Susannah said, not quite as huffily.

"You mean to tell me you don't remember those fake phone calls you made in front of Shania where you pretended to share gossip about Myrtle and Lill?"

"Who's Shania?"

"Your cleaner."

Wait! Susannah was the one who made up that story about my son and sent me that horrible card? Is that what Josephine's saying? I don't believe it, no I really, really don't.

"Why would I do such a thing?" Susannah said, stopping my roiling thoughts.

Indeed, why would she?

"An excellent question. Why would you? I don't know. But what I do know is you've caused distress to others in the past. Perhaps you do it because you're bored."

"If you're talking about my seeing you with that man in New York, I was just yanking your chain. I mean, I didn't tell your husband now, did I."

Josephine has a mysterious man in New

York? My goodness. Since she married Norman? No, no, it couldn't be. Susannah had to be talking about years ago. I've always wondered about Josephine's life before Brookside, because when she first arrived, she was clearly unhappy and not at all friendly. It took a major effort on my part to draw her out. In fact, without my help, I doubt she'd have a single friend to this day.

"Whether or not you told him, you held it over me," Josephine said. "In order to make me suffer, I suspect. Except I didn't, you see, because I didn't really care if you told. But you did hurt Myrtle with that story about her son. That was unkind. And what you concocted about Lill was downright wicked."

What Josephine was saying, that Susannah— my friend—that she was the source of that awful reminder of the worst thing that ever happened to me. No, she couldn't have done such a thing.

"You don't have a shred of proof," Susannah said.

"As a matter of fact, I do. In addition to Shania's report, do you remember the card you sent Myrtle? Well, I've had it tested. And it has your DNA on it."

Wait. Had what tested? The card? But I still have it. Then I remembered. Josephine had asked if she could have the envelope.

I'd opened that card in happy anticipation,

thinking it was a Christmas greeting, and when I'd seen what it was, I'd flung it away like it was a big hairy spider.

"And then there's that awful rumor you started about our police chief. You left a few fingerprints on that one as well."

What awful rumor about Mac? Oh, my. I had no idea what that could possibly be. If it's bad, it can't be true, of course. Mac is wonderful.

"So, here's what I think," Josephine was saying. "When I confronted you at Devi and Mac's Christmas party for snooping, it made you mad. Mad enough to do something to hurt me by hurting my friends."

Susannah tossed her head and shrugged. "I was just having some fun. Can't you people take a joke?"

"A joke! You think what you did was funny? You. Hurt. My. Friends."

My goodness, I don't believe I've ever seen Josephine so angry. And she wasn't the only one. As it sank in that Susannah had just confessed to being the one who sent me that card and started the rumor about my son, I was angry too.

And she hurt Lillian. And Mac. And she did it as a joke? What kind of person thinks something like that is funny? And all the time, she was pretending to be my friend, sitting across from me at almost every meal, acting as if butter wouldn't melt in her mouth.

Suddenly, I was so angry, I was having trouble catching my breath. How dare she.

"What you've done is despicable," Josephine said. "And if there are any more unpleasant rumors, I'm going to make sure you're evicted. Do I make myself clear?"

After a lengthy pause, Susannah nodded, and Josephine stood. "I'll leave you to contemplate your sins."

Josephine then glanced in my direction, giving me a quick nod before walking out. Susannah remained sitting, clutching her arms around herself and staring at the doorway.

There didn't seem to be a good reason to stay hidden any longer. I pulled my walker into position and stood up.

Susannah turned and gasped. "Oh. I didn't know anybody was here," she said. "Josephine and I were just having a chat."

She smiled, but I wasn't having it. She was not brushing me off.

"A chat. Really?" I expect Susannah was hoping I hadn't actually heard everything. But I had. "You said it was a joke. That you did it for fun." I straightened and stared at her, noticing for the first time her discontented expression and the sour lines that bracketed her mouth. And I wondered why I'd ever wanted her for a friend, let alone believed she was my friend. "My son's death was a joke to you?"

She stared back at me, her mouth working as if words were struggling to get out. "So. What if I did it?" was what finally emerged.

I realized my head was bobbing, why I was unsure. Maybe in acknowledgment of all the pieces that were clicking into place—what she'd done to me, to my friends. All except Mac. I had no idea what she'd done to him, but I'd find out. Not right this minute, though.

Because the memories of Robert that had been summoned for the second time overwhelmed me—the officer shifting from foot to foot as he told us about the accident right before we were to walk into the church for the wedding, Francie collapsing into a pile of white satin and tulle, sobbing, the looks on all the faces of our friends and family as the news spread.

No! I wasn't going back there. It was unbearable.

"Myrtle? Are you okay?"

I glanced at Susannah, who actually looked concerned, although I wondered if that was even possible given what I now knew about her. The answer was, thanks to her, I most definitely wasn't okay. But I didn't need to waste any more words on her. Josephine had taken care of that.

I pulled in a breath, turned, and walked away from her, leaning on my walker more heavily than

I had when I'd entered the room.

Chapter Twenty-Six

Josephine

After I left the library, I waited nearby for Myrtle to emerge. I worried that, in order to prove Susannah was the source of the rumor, I'd had to remind Myrtle yet again about the loss of her son.

And I could see when Myrtle stepped out of the library that I'd been right to worry. The look on her face stopped me from approaching her. She was suffering, and this time I'd been the cause, no matter my good intentions.

She shuffled past where I was sitting without acknowledging me. I wasn't even certain she was aware I was there. Reluctantly, I returned home, but found it difficult to settle. Finally, I called Lill and told her what I'd done.

"If you'd asked me, I would have said it sounded like a reasonable plan," Lill said. "You knew it would be impossible to convince Myrtle if she didn't hear a confession with her own ears."

"I just didn't realize how devastating it would be for her to discover her friend was actually a rat."

"Give her a little time," Lill said. "Then go see her. Do you want me to come with you?"

"No. I think this is something I need to do on my own."

I hung up, wondering how much time I needed to give Myrtle. An hour? A day? Finally, rather than continuing to worry, I mixed up a batch of cookies. I didn't consciously realize until I slid the first pan out of the oven that I was baking them for Myrtle.

As soon as the cookies cooled sufficiently, I packaged them up along with a box of oolong tea bags, hoping that would be enough to get Myrtle to listen to my apology. I knocked on her door and waited, knowing it might take her a minute or two to respond.

The door finally opened, and Myrtle, looking pale but calm, glanced from the plate of cookies to me. She sighed before stepping aside so I could come in.

Her apartment was as overstuffed with furniture and knickknacks as I remembered, and I could understand exactly what the housekeeper meant when she said it was a bear to clean.

"I want to apologize, Myrtle. I should have figured out another way to do that."

She shook her head and sighed again. "I

thought Glory did it. I was quite certain."

"I know you did. But Glory has no motive. Susannah does, even if it's a weird one."

"I still don't understand why she did it."

"I'm not sure even she can explain it. I brought tea. Would you like me to make you a cup?"

"That would be nice." Myrtle went over to the recliner and plopped down, and I could swear I heard the chair groan.

I walked past her into her tiny kitchen.

"But why doesn't Susannah like you?"

The kettle was handy. I added water and put it on to heat, then stepped back into the living room. "I really have no idea. I never did anything to her, at least that I know about. But I don't think she's ever liked me."

"I'm beginning to wonder if she even liked me. For sure she's not my friend."

"No, I'm not sure Susannah knows what it means to be a friend."

"I dare say you're right."

The kettle whistled. I pulled a couple of mugs out of the cupboard, poured the water, and added tea bags. I put several cookies on a small plate and set the mug and cookies within Myrtle's reach.

"What did she do to Mac?" Myrtle asked.

I told her about the internet post.

"Oh, that's dreadful. There really must be consequences."

I sipped tea and said nothing.

Looking thoughtful, Myrtle took a bite of cookie. "Okay. So, what do we do now?" she said after she polished off the cookie and some of the tea.

I shook my head. "I don't know that there's anything more we can or should do."

"I wonder if she feels any remorse."

"I don't know. And I am sorry," I said. "I wish it were someone else."

"Oh, don't fuss, Josephine. I think Susannah and I just fell into the habit of eating together. I'm not sure I ever really liked her, to tell you the truth, even before all this. I'll miss her kitty more than I will her."

"Still, I'm sorry."

She sighed. "Actually, she was a good distraction. Kept me from feeling too sorry for myself."

"Why are you feeling sorry for yourself?" I could have bitten my tongue, remembering Myrtle's son. She had every right to feel sorry for herself.

"You know. How it ended with Bertie. I know it's my own fault. I got caught up acting like I was still a Miss America contestant and, well, I probably took him for granted."

Probably? I had a brief memory of Myrtle before she started using the walker, leading Bertie in a merry dance. But now, well, wonders never cease. For Myrtle to both realize that's what she did and to admit it . . . all I can say is there's hope for the whole world.

"Being reminded of my son also reminded me that we never know how much time we're going to have, and we shouldn't waste any of it."

It surprised me that someone as old as Myrtle would need to be reminded of the passing of time. Just the simple fact she was well on her way to her nineties should suffice. But perhaps, like me, like most of us, she doesn't normally dwell on such things.

"You could apologize to Bertie," I said.

"Do you think that's a good idea?"

"I think it's entirely up to you. But usually, apologizing when we know we're in the wrong, it's good for the soul." And for sure, I wouldn't have been caught thinking or saying something like that pre-Brookside.

"It's not easy, though," Myrtle said.

"If it were easy, it wouldn't be as worthwhile, would it?"

"I expect not. But what if he just tells me to take a hike?"

"Invite him to go with you."

"Now, Josephine, don't think for one moment I don't know you're teasing me." She reached for another cookie.

"Bottom line, you have nothing to lose, except maybe your dignity, but you could gain back a friend. Not to mention someone other than Susannah to eat dinner with."

"I hate to admit you're probably right, but then, you usually are."

I thought that was an excellent note on which to end the visit.

~ ~ ~

"I succeeded in sticking a spoke in Susannah's wheel, and I convinced Myrtle of her guilt," I told Norman at dinner that evening.

"And you sound gleeful about it," Norman said.

"Maybe a little gleeful, but also relieved." I told him how I'd staged the conversation so Myrtle would overhear.

"What's Myrtle going to do with the information?"

"We didn't actually talk about that. But I think Susannah is definitely in the rearview mirror as far as Myrtle's concerned. The whole episode has her thinking about trying to reconcile with

Bertie."

"O . . . kay. Did not see that coming."

"She said that remembering her son reminded her we never know how much time we have."

"Too true. Although, I've never considered Myrtle a philosopher."

"Today, for at least a few minutes, in between cookies, she was."

"So, do you have other plans for Susannah?"

"I'm still thinking about it."

~ ~ ~

Christmas, the Girls' Night Out, and New Years had all passed without Charlie Culpepper trying to get in touch with Richard through the JLR fund website, and we were all beginning to feel that the plan had somehow crashed and burned. But then Roxanne Culpepper called and invited us to dinner.

"Charlie and I have decided we want to spread our wings this year and get to know as many of our fellow residents as possible. We'd like another couple to join us as well. We were thinking that perhaps Richard . . . do you think he and . . . is he married, by the way?"

"He is."

"Well, do you think that perhaps he and his wife would be willing to join the four of us for dinner at . . .?" She named a very elegant and expensive restaurant. "Our treat, of course."

She said she'd take care of reservations if I'd let her know about Richard.

"I know I shouldn't speak for Richard and Philippa without checking, but I know they've wanted to meet some new people as well. I'm sure they'll be delighted to be included."

I also knew the four of us would insist on paying our own way, but that was something we could hash out at the restaurant.

We concluded the call with me promising to let her know which of the dates she proposed would work for Richard, whom I called immediately.

"Outstanding. The con is on," was Richard's response.

We fixed on a date, and I called Roxanne back. She professed herself rapturous at the news.

I hung up, shaking my head.

~ ~ ~

Norman drove, and Richard and Philippa rode with us to the restaurant. As planned, we arrived a few minutes late in order to give Charlie and Roxanne time to arrive and get settled.

"Oh, I know you," Roxanne exclaimed when Philippa was introduced. "Someone told me you're a writer."

"I am," Philippa said, taking a seat.

"What do you write?" Charlie asked, sounding, to my ears, not really interested.

"Novels." Philippa must have picked up on his lack of sincere interest as well, but even in the best of times, Philippa is a woman of few spoken words. She saves them for her books. And her friends. And we all knew the Culpeppers would never be that.

"Very entertaining novels," I said. "Based on some of the adventures we've all had since moving into Brookside."

"Loosely based," Philippa said, smiling at me.

"Oh, I do want to hear more about that," Roxanne said, glancing first at Philippa and then at me.

A waiter arrived and, after greeting us, stood at the ready to take our drink orders. Roxanne and Charlie ordered martinis, and Richard, as was our habit, picked out a moderately priced bottle of wine for the four of us to share.

"So, you're enjoying Brookside," I said when all the initial flurries had settled down and we'd clinked glasses and wished each other a healthy and prosperous new year.

"Oh, we are," Roxanne said. "And it's not easy to find a place where one feels so comfortable and in tune with one's fellow residents."

"Have you tried someplace else, then?" I said.

"Actually . . ." She glanced at Charlie, who nodded slightly. "We did take advantage of The Springs' offer. They let you live in a furnished apartment for a couple of months to see if you want to move in permanently."

"I see you're sticking with an aquatic theme," Richard said.

"Aquatic theme?"

"The Springs, Brookside."

"Oh, I see what you mean. Well, not on purpose."

"So, you decided you didn't like The Springs?" I said.

"We just didn't feel quite at home there, did we, Charlie?"

"Not like Brookside," Charlie agreed.

The waiter came over, and Roxanne and Charlie ordered refills on their martinis. The rest of us looked at our menus, and the next few minutes were occupied with deciding and ordering. Salads and appetizers arrived promptly. As we ate, the conversation fell into the usual get-acquainted patterns. We gave the weather its due attention and offered each other platitudes about our Christmas celebrations, the losing Bengals' football season, and hopes for better luck with the baseball season in the spring. By the time dessert was being ordered, I was beginning to think we'd misjudged the Culpeppers' motives for inviting us.

Roxanne, on her third martini, insisted we had to try the dessert soufflés. That meant a twenty-minute hiatus between our dinner plates being cleared and the desserts arriving.

Charlie took full advantage of that time to grill Richard to well-done perfection on his investing experiences over the years.

As he did so, the rest of us sat, mostly silent, stretching out our last sips of wine.

"It's actually been a sideline of mine," Richard said. "But it's turned out to be more lucrative than my original career."

"Oh, what was that?" Charlie asked.

"I was a salesman," Richard said.

I covered my smile by taking a sip of water. Salesman was an excellent synonym for con man.

"Investing has been a sideline of mine as well," Charlie said, "on a strictly amateur basis, you understand. I must say I was fascinated by what Mrs. . . . what's her name again, honey?"

"Grabinowitz," Roxanne supplied.

"Yes, Mrs. Grabinowitz. What she told

Roxanne about her recent financial report. And she said you were the one who'd advised her?"

Actually, Myrtle had told Roxanne I was responsible with help from Richard, but it was clear that Charlie was one of those men who only believed what another man had to say. Norman reached for my hand under the table and squeezed it. He knew that sort of thing annoys me and was just reminding me to keep the big picture in mind. I squeezed back, message received.

"The fund was actually Jo's discovery," Richard said, smiling at me. It was obvious he had also picked up on Charlie's proclivity to discount my contributions. "That is, if you're talking about the JLR fund?"

"I do believe that's what Mrs. Grabinowitz called it, wasn't it, hon?"

Roxanne gave him a slightly glassy look. He casually reached for her drink and took a sip before setting it down out of her reach. It was done with the élan of long practice. She glared at him.

He looked back at Richard, and I wondered if either of the Culpeppers realized that we would know that the only way they could know the name of the fund was if they'd snooped into the contents of the envelope. Which, of course, they had.

Roxanne tapped Charlie's hand and motioned

at the drink. He picked it up and took another swallow before handing the nearly empty glass back to her.

Philippa and I exchanged a glance. Charlie, ignoring Roxanne, got back to his conversation with Richard.

"I've been thinking about moving some of our funds into something with a better yield, and I've been on the lookout for something precisely like this. I'm hoping you can tell me a bit more about this fund."

"Well, for starters, the buy-in is half a million minimum," Richard said. "Are you still interested?"

"Absolutely."

Roxanne sat back, looking annoyed while Richard went into the details he'd concocted about the fund. According to him, it has consistently out-performed more venerable funds like Berkshire Hathaway, and it had even held its value with the recent downturn.

"I can attest to that," I said.

Charlie glanced at me only briefly before returning his attention to Richard. I looked at Norman, whose lips twitched in amusement. For sure, we were going to enjoy knocking Charlie down a peg or three.

"So, who do I get in touch with to arrange a

buy-in?" Charlie asked.

"Well, that could be a problem," Richard said. "I can share a copy of the prospectus with you, but the fund administrator is quite picky about who's allowed to invest."

It was then, with perfect timing, two waiters arrived, carrying soufflés that they set down in front of us with a flourish. Roxanne and Charlie each had their own, but the four of us were sharing the remaining two.

"You'll be sorry," Roxanne had warned us.

She gestured at her glass, asking for a refill, but Charlie placed his hand over it and shook his head at the waiter.

"So, besides the five hundred thousand minimum, what else do I need to do?"

"Actually, the buy-in may have gone up. I'd have to check. But JLR doesn't take any money until they're satisfied the investor is legit. The administrator doesn't want to get caught up in helping crooks make even more money from their ill-gotten gains."

I almost choked on a bite of soufflé. I coughed, and Charlie glanced at me before returning his attention to Richard. Roxanne was right. The soufflé, the part I hadn't just inhaled, was delicious.

"While I'm pretty sure you're on the up and up," Richard said, dividing his attention between Charlie and the soufflé he was sharing with

Philippa, "the fund manager won't just take my word for it. I'm pretty small potatoes, you see."

It hit me what Richard was doing. He was using a classic denial technique to make Charlie even more determined to be allowed to buy in.

"So if he won't take your word, what do I need to do?"

I loved that while Richard hadn't disclosed the fund manager's gender, Charlie had made his own assumptions.

"Be a start if you can convince her," Richard said with a lazy swoop of his spoon toward me. "After all, she's the one who vouched for me and for Mrs. Grabinowitz."

Suddenly, I had all of Charlie's attention.

"We'd sure appreciate your help with this," he said.

I'd be willing to bet that before Richard's statement, Charlie couldn't have even said what color outfit I was wearing, and I wasn't entirely certain he remembered my name. I was also pretty sure Richard was playing with Charlie like a cat does a mouse. Unfortunately, he'd now tossed that somewhat battered mouse at me.

"What is it I need to do?" Charlie said, giving me an intense look from under his Andy Rooney eyebrows.

I didn't have a clue. But I couldn't very well

say that.

"To start with, I'll need access to your credit report and verification from your bank that you have the necessary funds," I said, winging it.

"I can help you with organizing all that," Richard offered. "I know how busy you are, Jo, so if you'd like me . . .?"

"Excellent. You're right. I really don't have time to do a full audit right now, but you know what's needed," I said, tossing the ball-mouse back at Richard.

"Tell you what," Richard said. "Why don't we meet next Tuesday and get everything squared away so I can let Jo know it's all copasetic and she can inform JLR of your interest."

"Sure. Okay. Sounds good," Charlie said.

At that point, I relaxed and enjoyed the last bites of the dessert, since the main purpose of the evening seemed to have been accomplished.

The waiter returned and asked if we wanted separate checks and Charlie started to say yes to that, but Roxanne tapped him on the arm and smiled at the waiter. "Just bring us the check," she said.

Norman and Richard put up token resistance, but Charlie waved their offers aside. Reluctantly, I diagnosed. But it was a smart move on his part if he wanted our help with the investment.

As soon as the bill was settled, we said our goodnights

"Well, wasn't that special," Philippa said, as we arrived back at the car. "So much money, so little enjoyment."

"I disagree," I said. "We just had an outstandingly delicious meal with two of our favorite people, and yes, there was the occasional interruption from two other people who are definitely not our favorites, but on balance it was a nice evening."

"Besides, it gave us a chance to further sink the hook into Charlie," Norman said. "And now that he's subsidized an expensive meal, he's going to be even more eager to get approved to invest in JLR."

"In other words, we've just taken a bribe," I said.

"Pretty much."

"You are going to take his money," I said to Richard.

"I certainly am," Richard said.

"Good, because you almost gave me a heart attack when you made that pivot to me."

"But wasn't it fun tweaking his little gender inequality gene," Richard said. "Besides, it's true. You're by far the most talented investor I know, but I'm the better scammer. Don't worry. I have some ideas of what to put him through before I tell him you've given him the royal Josephine imprimatur. I intend to make him beg me to take his money."

"Good luck with that," I said.

"Luck isn't even part of the equation," Richard said.

~ ~ ~

I was finishing a cup of tea and chatting with Glory, who had stopped by on one of her brief visits. I asked about her friend.

"I'm hoping she'll hang on long enough to know if your plan works," Glory said.

"We should know by the end of the week," I told her.

There was a knock on the door. I answered to find Susannah standing there.

"Josephine, I need to speak to you. I hope now's okay?"

She sounded and looked so rattled, I didn't have the heart to close the door in her face, although that was what I was tempted to do.

Glory stepped behind me. "Susannah, good to see you. I better get back, Josephine. Talk to you soon."

Glory left, although I would have preferred her to stay. I closed the door behind her and led Susannah into the living room, where she took a seat across from me, her hands in her lap, clenching and unclenching.

I raised an eyebrow in question.

"That conversation we had a while back? Myrtle heard us."

"Yes, I know. I asked her to be there."

She glanced at me, apparently startled. "Why?"

"You were pretending to be her friend. She needed to know what you were capable of, and she wouldn't have believed me otherwise. You see, Myrtle is very loyal to those she considers friends."

Susannah sat there blinking, and a pause developed that was making me feel as uncomfortable as she looked.

She lifted her chin and took a breath. "I shouldn't have done what I did."

"Are you sorry? Or just sorry you were caught?"

"I'm sorry about Myrtle. She's been a good friend, and I've never had many of those."

"Maybe now you know why."

She chewed on her lip before looking at me. "I didn't realize it would go this far. I mean, they were all just experiments. Pranks, I suppose. I didn't mean to hurt her."

"What about Lill? And Mac?"

"No, I shouldn't have done those things either."

"You need to make sure they know that."

"I, I don't know if I can."

I didn't respond to that.

Finally, she sighed. "I never liked you, you know."

"I know. I just don't know why."

"Because of Thomas. I saw how you treated him. And he was . . . he didn't deserve that indifference. And even though you didn't care about him, you refused to divorce him." She stopped, tears filling her eyes.

Wow! So Susannah did have a relationship with Thomas. One that was serious enough for talk of divorce. I would have granted it, gladly, but there was nothing to be gained by telling her that now. I did debate whether to tell her how much more than indifference Thomas had deserved but then decided she wouldn't believe me.

She swiped at her eyes and firmed her lips. "I'm sorry I caused your friends difficulties. They all seem like nice people."

"They are."

"So you'll let Myrtle know I met with you."

"And spoke sincerely and honestly," I said, not trying to be ironic, although that might be how it sounded. "Yes, I'll tell her. It won't change things, though, if that's what you're hoping."

Her shoulders slumped, and for an instant, I thought it was possible she did regret what she'd done.

"I guess I'll be going now."

"Yes. I think that's best."

I followed her to the door, then watched as she headed back to the main building, head bent, clutching her coat around her, looking diminished from the Cruella de Vil version of herself at Christmas.

I surprised myself by feeling a preference for her Cruella incarnation. It seemed I was more comfortable opposing a strong, unpleasant version of Susannah, than a beaten, sad one. At the same time, I was relieved I no longer needed to worry about what she might choose to do to hurt someone else I cared about.

Chapter Twenty-Seven

Devi

"I had a most peculiar and unexpected visitor today," Mac said as we were feeding the twins.

Nick had picked Mika up earlier and was keeping her for the next couple of days, so it was just the twins, Mac, and me, for the first time in nearly a week.

"Oh," I said, aiming a spoonful of peas at Lily's eager mouth, glad of any distraction. I was missing Mika.

"Yeah. Susannah Rasmussen. She came to offer an apology."

"Ah."

"You know about this?"

"Maybe. Why don't you tell me."

"Okay. She's the one who wrote that social media post that caused us so much difficulty. In fact, we're still addressing some of the fallout."

"Are you? You haven't mentioned it."

"It's mostly down to the occasional phone call seeking additional information about the police chief's fancy house."

I had the distinct feeling that was a euphemism for some highly unpleasant interactions with irate, poorly informed Montgomery residents, but I didn't want to force Mac to relive any of it.

"Was it a good apology?"

He grimaced. "It was certainly abject. I think she was quite concerned I might have grounds to arrest her."

"And do you? Have grounds, that is."

"If we chased after everyone who posts lies on the internet, I'd need to triple my force and we'd still have no time to do anything else."

"Did you tell her that?"

"Absolutely not. Hopefully, I left her with the impression I was thinking about it."

"Good. She's a dreadful woman."

"I feel kind of sorry for her."

"Why?"

"My theory is that she has a very serious case of Jo envy, and it's eating away at her."

"Did she tell you that?"

"Not in so many words. But it's pretty clear from everything she did. I got the feeling it had to do with Jo's luck in husbands."

"Not so lucky," I said. "Josephine's first husband was a nightmare."

"You're saying he abused her?"

"Not physically, but for sure, he was an emotional abuser. I guess I can understand Susannah envying Josephine, not because of the men in her life, but rather because Josephine is an amazing person, and Susannah most definitely isn't."

"The other funny thing is that she asked me to please let Myrtle know she'd apologized and taken full responsibility for her actions."

"Oh good. It's working, then."

"What is?"

"Josephine told Susannah that if she didn't apologize, personally and sincerely, to everyone she hurt, Josephine would make sure the entire Brookside community finds out what she's done."

"So why did I have to report to Myrtle?"

"Josephine thinks Susannah is trying to repair the relationship."

"Well, it doesn't seem to be working. When I called Myrtle to report, she thanked me, but she didn't sound very enthusiastic."

"I don't think she is. You'll have to agree it's pretty hard to make amends for that kind of thing."

"I have to give Susannah some credit, though. It wasn't easy to come speak to me."

"So maybe she's trying to change. But she has a long way to go."

"Well, don't forget, Edna managed it."

"Edna just helped herself to things," I said. "Susannah hurt people."

"You're right. She does have a lot of work to do."

"That she does."

Chapter Twenty-Eight

Josephine

Richard called to let us know he'd been notified by the bank that the Culpepper check had cleared and the funds had been deposited in a special trust account.

This news came after Richard had led Charlie Culpepper in a delicate dance for over two weeks, enticing Charlie's interest, but then informing him he likely wouldn't qualify as an investor. That had led to a visit from Roxanne who, woman to woman, begged me to intervene. At that point, Richard knew it was time for the final push that today had resulted in this excellent news.

Richard suggested we invite the Culpeppers over that evening so he could explain the fine print in the contract they'd signed when they turned over the check.

"Ask him if we should invite Mac," I told Norman.

"He says why not," Norman said when he finished the call. "He's also suggesting we include Glory."

"Of course, she has to be here. After all, she's the one who started this off."

~ ~ ~

In the end, we also included Myrtle and Edna, since they'd played an important part in baiting the hook, so to speak. And Philippa and Devi were definitely not going to sit this one out.

Everyone other than the Culpeppers arrived at seven to give Richard time to brief us all about what had transpired. He let Glory speak first, and she explained for those who didn't know how she'd discovered that the Culpeppers, AKA the Carpenters, were scam artists.

"I thought for sure the bad guy was Andrew Winston," Myrtle said, in a completely predictable way. "Even when you said you were also looking at Charlie and Roxanne. But after you said that, when Bertie said Charlie had talked to him about an investment, I warned him to be careful. Although that was after I saw with my own eyes how unpleasant Charlie had been to Martha and Mary. So I would have been suspicious, anyway."

I shook my head. Myrtle had once again managed to be in the middle of the action even when the rest of us were unaware of it, and trust me, Myrtle rarely flies under the radar.

"Good thing you warned Bertie," Richard said. "And Jo was the one who made sure Martha and Mary didn't lose their money."

"Well, I say good for me and for you,

Josephine," Myrtle said.

With all the interruptions, I worried that Richard wouldn't get through all the explanations before the Culpeppers arrived.

Richard cleared his throat, and Myrtle's mouth snapped shut. Finally.

"So, what we've done is to arrange for the Culpeppers to make a large contribution to the recovery fund that will be used to pay back as many of their victims as we can locate."

"But how did you manage that?" Myrtle said. "I'm quite sure they wouldn't do that willingly."

"After the three of you engaged Charlie's interest with your little act in the dining room, I was subsequently able to convince him that the JLR fund was the greatest thing since jet travel. And then I made it seem even more attractive by making it selective and telling him I doubted he would qualify as an investor. That made him so eager to write me a check, I doubt I could have restrained him if I'd wanted to. And I didn't."

"So this J something-or-other fund actually exists?" Myrtle asked.

"JLR. But not in the form the Culpeppers assume. Not an investment fund, but a trust fund."

"What does the JLR stand for?" Myrtle asked.

"Josephine, Lillian, Richard," Norman said.

"Oh. Well, I certainly would have been more than happy to lend an initial," Myrtle said. "I think JLMR has rather a nice ring."

It did, actually. Not that a one of us was going to admit it.

"Bottom line, in all my comments about the fund, I made it clear the money could just as easily disappear as it could yield substantial returns, and I talked about the fund's charitable arm."

As Richard spoke, I watched Mac for any sign his dedication to upholding the law was being compromised. He simply sat, sipping his Scotch with a thoughtful look.

The doorbell rang, and I went and ushered in the Culpeppers.

"My goodness," Roxanne said. "You have quite a crowd. Did we get the time wrong?"

"No, not at all. We just had some business to conduct first. I believe you know most of us, but perhaps you haven't yet met our chief of police?"

I led them over to Mac and made the introductions. Charlie, who had a reasonably smooth social persona, appeared to hesitate as he shook Mac's hand.

I didn't bother to offer them drinks. For one thing, I didn't think they'd be around that long, and for another, I knew we would soon be dealing with two very unhappy people.

Conversation died down as Mac greeted the

Culpeppers, and then Richard once again took the floor.

"We're glad you could join us, Charlie, Roxanne, because we're celebrating something you made a very large contribution to."

The two stood, looking quizzical.

"But before we go into that, I'm thinking we should first make sure you meet Glory Pennycutt."

"Don't believe I've had the pleasure," Charlie said as Richard gestured toward where Glory sat next to Lill.

"No, I didn't think you had," Richard said. "But I do believe you're acquainted with Glory's very good friend, Dorothy Freid. Dorothy, until recently, was a resident of The Springs, where you also resided, briefly, I believe?"

"No. Sorry. I don't I know a Dorothy Freid," Charlie said, his glance beginning to dart around the room.

"But you don't deny that you lived for a short time at The Springs?"

Charlie started blinking very fast, and Roxanne moved closer to him.

"And while there, you scammed Dorothy and two of her friends out of $130,000 by talking them into investing in a bogus company that almost immediately went bust. That was you, wasn't it?"

"Of course it wasn't."

"Oh, that's right. My bad. It was someone named Carpenter who bilked Dorothy. Isn't that what you told us, Glory?"

"It was. However, I also told you I thought the Culpeppers bear a remarkable resemblance to the Carpenters."

"Yes, indeed you did, and they do." Richard turned to pick up photographs sitting on the mantelpiece.

"I'll just pass these around, shall I? These were provided by Dorothy's friends at The Springs, who identified the couple pictured here as Roxanne and Chuck Carpenter. Further, they say that it was this couple who scammed them out of fifteen thousand dollars each."

Richard handed off the pictures and again looked at the Culpeppers. "We'd be happy to entertain any explanation you'd care to offer."

Charlie simply shook his head. Roxanne grabbed at his hand, but he batted her away.

I felt a twinge of sympathy for Roxanne, but then I reminded myself that she'd chosen, along with Charlie, to scam the elderly and the terminally ill.

"Okay. So, no explanation then. That's your right. Not to incriminate yourself. Especially in the presence of the chief of police."

Charlie's Adam's apple bobbed. "We're leaving," he said. He grabbed Roxanne's hand and turned toward the door. Norman stepped over to the door, his hand out to open it.

"You're free to go, of course," he said. "But I think it's best if you stay. I think you'll find the rest even more fascinating. Here, let me get you a seat."

He collected a couple of chairs from the dining room and set them down near Charlie and Roxanne. Charlie looked around the room, and then, without a word, sat down. Roxanne was no longer attempting to hold his hand, and both their complexions looked pasty.

"What have you done, Charlie?" Roxanne said, her voice high-pitched and skittery.

"What do you mean, what have I done?" He appeared to be both angry and frightened. A potentially dangerous combination. I was suddenly glad Mac was there.

"I don't do anything without you playing your part," Charlie said with a glare at Roxanne. "So just say what you have to say," he said, turning the glare on Richard.

"Happy to," Richard said. "After Glory came to us with her concerns, I took those concerns to our police chief." He nodded at Mac. "And Mac was able to check on things I would have had difficulty finding out. He discovered that what we were dealing with involved both fake identities and financial scams, and that you've committed these crimes at three retirement communities, and perhaps more. He was also able to track down several victims of the scam at The Springs while we, with Glory's help, identified potential victims here at Brookside. I then worked to get you to do the right thing and return the money you'd stolen."

Some of what Richard was saying was news to me, the part about working with Mac, for instance, but really it shouldn't have been a surprise. I glanced at Norman and decided from the look on his face that he might not have known all the details either. And that better be true or he'd be dealing with explaining why he'd let me worry we were operating slightly outside the law, when all the time we were snugly within its boundaries.

"The worse thing about what you've done," Richard said, "is that you've targeted the elderly, because you know they're the most likely to fall for your dishonest schemes. That's truly reprehensible."

"It certainly is," Myrtle said. "Reprehensible."

I think Richard giving her some of the credit for hooking Charlie had gone to her head.

"So, JLR," Charlie said. His tone was both angry and resigned. "I take it, it's not what you represented it to be."

"Your check cleared, by the way," Richard said.

"Money you took under false pretenses," Charlie said.

"Not at all. Did you not read the contract you signed? And you must remember me telling you that one aspect of the fund was its charitable arm?"

Charlie bent his head and clenched and unclenched his hands. I had the distinct feeling he wanted to jump up and throttle Richard. Again, I was glad Mac was there, although Charlie's not that big, so either Richard or Norman could likely subdue him.

"I assure you, I gave you every opportunity to reach a full understanding of what you were doing, both in what I said to you and what was in the contract."

"You manipulated me."

"Yeah, okay. That's probably a fair assessment. But I think you'll have to agree, not precisely in the way you manipulated Dorothy and her friends and tried to manipulate Bertie, Martha, and Mary."

"I'll sue you," Charlie said, but the words were resigned.

"Yes, well, that's your right. And now, we have some checks to distribute," Richard said.

"Jo, will you give me a hand?"

He turned to the mantle once again where several envelopes were sitting. "This first check goes to the Dorothy Freid trust," Richard said. He handed me the envelope, and I carried it over to Glory.

Glory's eyes teared up. She turned and looked at the Culpeppers. "When you took this money from Dorothy, you were actually stealing her granddaughter's future." Then she looked from me to Norman to Richard. "I simply can't find adequate words to tell you how much I appreciate what you've done for my friend and her family."

"How is she doing?" Lill asked.

"It won't be long. Not now. But this felt like unfinished business to her. It will bring her a great deal of peace to know her granddaughter is taken care of. Elizabeth is the most important person in the world to Dorothy, and she was distraught when she discovered a big chunk of the money she wanted Elizabeth to have was gone."

"As for these other envelopes"—Richard held them up and fanned them out—"they contain checks made out to the other victims we've been able to identify. Mac will see that they get to their proper owners."

"Is there anything left?" Myrtle asked.

"As a matter of fact," Richard said, "since Charlie absolutely insisted on a larger buy-in than five hundred thousand, we have nearly two hundred thousand left over."

"What happens to it?" Myrtle said.

"The money will be held in trust for two years as we continue to search for additional victims. After two years, anything left will be donated to charity, and the trust dissolved."

"What you did was illegal," Charlie said. "And you've just admitted it in front of a cop." He turned to Mac. "Why don't you arrest him for theft? He stole seven hundred and fifty thousand dollars from me."

Mac shook his head. "You freely wrote that check and insisted that Richard accept it. I've seen video evidence of the transaction."

"You can't record me without my permission. That's entrapment."

"Actually, in Ohio, recordings are legal as long as one of the parties knows they're being recorded."

"Well. Well. That's. That's . . ."

"I agree," Mac said. "That's excellent work on Richard's part."

"I'm done here. Come on, Roxanne. We're leaving."

"I'm afraid I can't let you leave," Mac said. "You're under arrest, and since I'm concerned that you're flight risks, you'll have to be in custody until you're arraigned."

Mac lifted his phone to his ear and spoke briefly. A minute later, there was a knock on our door. Norman opened it to one of Mac's officers. He'd arrived so promptly it was clear that Mac had arranged for him to wait outside for his signal.

Mac spoke briefly with the officer, who then accompanied the Culpeppers out the door. The rest of us took a collective deep breath.

"Well, my goodness," Myrtle said. "That was exciting."

Exciting and sad. But also satisfying to know we'd stopped the Culpeppers in their tracks and recovered a big chunk of what they'd stolen from their elderly victims.

Chapter Twenty-Nine

Devi

In early February, Mac called me at work to warn me that Nick would be coming over this evening, possibly with news about Lisa.

"We'll need to get dinner out of the way early, so I'll stop at the Tandoor for takeout," he said.

One of the things I love about Mac is that whenever our lives get complicated, he suggests takeout—a gift to me, since I do most of the cooking.

At home, we worked together, as we always did, to feed, bathe, and settle the twins for the night. They must have sensed something was up, because they were a bit more bouncy than usual, but we finally tiptoed out of their room with twenty minutes' leeway to finish our own dinners before Nick was due to arrive.

When he did, he wasn't alone. He had Lisa with him. And Mika, of course. It was the first time I'd seen Lisa since before she was hospitalized, and I confess, I was nervous. Nick bustled about, helping Lisa with her coat and then taking Mika from her to follow us into the family room.

Mac told Lisa it was great to see her. He even leaned in and kissed her on the cheek. I expect he was expressing some of the relief I was feeling that Lisa seemed calm and together, in a way I'm not sure she'd ever been before, in her interactions with me.

"Can I see Lily and Toby?" she asked, sounding tentative.

"They're asleep," I said, but then noticing her expression, I added, "You can look in on them if you like."

"Oh, yes, please," she said.

I went with her and was relieved when she didn't insist on turning on a light. She stood in the doorway for a time, just looking, and then she turned to me with a smile.

"You're a wonderful mother, Devi. I can see what good care you take of them. The way you love them."

My heart hitched. Was there a *but* coming? *But, I'm their real mother, and I want them back.* At least while she'd been hospitalized I'd had no worries about that, but I realized, watching her now, that the worry never truly left. The thought that one day she might swoop in and demand custody.

"I'm so grateful to you and Darren, you know." As she spoke, we started back downstairs.

"I'm glad you're feeling better. You are, aren't you?"

"I am."

By that time, we reached the room where Nick and Mac were chatting. Both had glasses of Scotch they were sipping, Nick with Mika nestled in his arms.

Lisa walked over to Nick and sat down beside him. He set his glass down and curled an arm around her. I was very glad to see that. I took a seat near Mac.

Nick and Lisa exchanged a look, and she nodded.

"We came tonight to let you know what we've

decided about the future," Nick said. "Lisa is doing great, but she has to be very careful about stress for the foreseeable future. That means she won't be returning to Japan."

Uh-oh. My stomach clenched in anticipation of his next words.

"I'll be returning there for a short time to help the new person settle in and to pack up our things, but after that, I'll be back here permanently."

Wow! Okay, thank goodness. I reached for Mac's hand, and he took mine in his and squeezed reassuringly.

"That sounds like excellent news," Mac said.

"It is," Nick said.

"When do you go back?" I asked.

"In about a month. Meanwhile, we've already hired a daytime nanny for Michelle, and we've started looking for a house."

"Don't you have a house?" I asked.

"We signed a long-term rental agreement for while we were away. So we've decided to look for another place, probably in Hyde Park. I really like the idea of cutting down on my commute."

"That all sounds great," I said, trying not to sound as relieved as I was feeling.

"I want to thank you both," Lisa said. She stopped and bit her lip. "I had no idea how sick I was, and you, you stepped in and made sure Michelle was taken care of, and, well . . . I'll never, ever be able to pay you back."

"No need," I spoke quickly, trying to help her fight off the tears I could see gathering in her eyes.

She'd already paid us back two times over when she allowed us to adopt the twins. I know that Mac and Josephine have both assured me Lisa can't reverse that arrangement, but every time she shows up, I worry she might try. So this new version of Lisa was a relief for two reasons. First, it sounded like she had no intention of trying to take the twins away from us, and second, I didn't have to worry about Mika being in Lisa's care. And I realized as that thought expanded my chest with a deep breath, that I had been worrying about that quite a lot.

This didn't mean, of course, that there wouldn't be times in the future when we might clash with Lisa over the upbringing of the twins, but with Nick keeping a close eye on her and with her hands full raising Mika, I thought we'd all be okay.

I realized as I pulled in another breath that I hadn't breathed freely without the feeling a dark cloud was gathering ever since Lisa returned from Japan. What a blessed, blessed relief this news was.

This was the special Christmas I'd been

hoping for. It simply arrived a few weeks later than expected.

Chapter Thirty

Josephine

We hadn't heard from Glory for several days when I saw the obituary for her friend in the newspaper. I called and invited her for dinner that evening and invited Lill as well.

Glory arrived, along with a swirl of late snow and puffs of crisp air.

"We were so sorry to see the news about your friend," I said, as I hung up her coat.

"Please, don't be. Dorothy was ready to go, and Elizabeth was with her at the end."

"I'm so glad to hear that," I said.

"What's difficult is that these past couple of months, I've gotten up every day knowing I was going to spend most of it with Dorothy, so I'm really missing her."

"You'll have more time for us," Lill said.

Glory smiled, but it was a half-hearted effort

at best.

"Not for long," she said.

"Why is that?" I asked.

"I'm moving out of Brookside. The end of the month."

"But why? I thought you liked it here," Lill said.

"I do, and I really like all of you. Well, most of you. I think you'll agree to my exempting Susannah, the Culpeppers, and the Winstons from that list."

"There's a rumor the Winstons are leaving, too," Norman said. The Culpeppers were already gone.

"Why?" Lill said, sounding startled.

"Marge had a talk with them about the petition to get rid of you. It made them both spitting furious. We can only hope they don't renege on their promise to leave this 'unfriendly, autocratic, unpleasant, masquerading-as-a-community place.'"

"See, Glory," Lill said. "Brookside has just been further improved upon. With the Winstons gone, it's only Susannah you have to avoid. You simply can't leave."

Glory sighed. "The truth is, I only moved here to try to catch the Culpeppers. I could never afford to live here long term."

"Where do you live?" I asked.

"I have a house. In Blue Ash. And although the mortgage is paid off, the housing market is bubkis right now, as you probably know."

I did. With the downturn in the economy, lots of people were losing their homes or going underwater on mortgages.

"Do you like living at Brookside?" I asked.

"I do, actually. I didn't know what to expect, and of course I had an ulterior motive for being here, but meeting all of you has been a real gift."

"So if it were possible to live here, would you?" I said, just to be certain.

"I would. But woulda coulda aside, I can't. It's going to be lonely going back to my house, though. I never felt alone before, you know. But now, I expect I just need to get a job. Save up until the market improves, sell my house, and see what I can manage then."

"What kind of job would you look for?" I asked, a thought beginning to niggle in the back of my mind.

"I was the house manager for a prominent family for years. That's how I met Dorothy. She was their secretary, but that was a few years ago. Eventually, the young ones grew up and moved away, and the parents died. Since then, I've held admin positions different places, and I don't mind that. It's not as personal as a position with a family, but it pays the bills. Luckily, I'd just left my last position when Dorothy told me what had happened to her."

"Well, we're going to miss you. Me especially," Lill said. "You do realize that was a pretty amazing thing you did for your friend, moving in here to stop the Culpeppers."

"I didn't tell Dorothy all of that," Glory said, her face turning pink. "But I just couldn't stand seeing her being taken advantage of. Not after she worked so hard for that money."

"We're so grateful you told us about it," Lill said. "Josephine and I do love adventures."

When the evening ended, it was with hugs all around and resolutions to spend as much time as we could with each other in the future.

Chapter Thirty-One

Lillian

Josephine gave me a very generous gift certificate to my favorite hat shop for Christmas, and now was the perfect time to go shopping for a new spring hat. It was also a way to break the monotony that had followed in the wake of our

Winston, Culpepper, and Susannah adventures.

I invited Josephine to go with me and suggested we invite Maddie, Devi, and Glory to join us, since it's always more fun shopping with friends.

The hat "shop" is really an apartment in the Over the Rhine part of downtown Cincinnati, and the hatmaker, one Vivienne, is available only by appointment. I arranged that, and on a Saturday in late February, the five of us arrived, right on time.

I hadn't bought a new hat in years, but Vivienne greeted me as if we were long-lost sisters. She seated us and served tea and tiny cookies—Myrtle would have been disappointed—and as we sat sipping and nibbling, she showed us her new designs. I immediately fell in love with a pale green hat, and I knew the lavender one would be perfect for Josephine. I nodded my head toward Josephine, and Vivienne came over and placed the hat on her head.

"Oh my, oh my," Vivienne said, standing back. "Must have had a vision. That hat simply will not be happy on anybody else's head."

"But I never wear hats," Josephine said.

"You should, though," Devi said. "You look amazing."

"I don't believe I've ever looked amazing in my life," Josephine said. And I could tell she wasn't fishing for a compliment. She really believed it. She started to lift the hat off her head, but Vivienne took her by the hand and led her over to a mirror.

"You see, lovey, this hat belongs to you, and only you," Vivienne said, standing off to the side.

"It's lovely, but it would be a shame to buy it and then just leave it in my closet," Josephine said, turning toward us.

"Oh, it won't stand for that," Vivienne said. "That hat's going to make sure it gets out. Trust me."

"I can think of one possibility," Devi said, a hand discreetly pointing at Maddie. Then she quickly placed her finger over her lips, motioning for us not to say anything. Maddie didn't notice, thank goodness. But I knew what Devi was hinting. That someday soon there might be a wedding. Maddie and Oliver's. When that happens, I plan to be the one to walk Maddie down the aisle, since she has no other family. Except all of us, of course.

"Oh," Josephine said, before she could stop herself. "Perhaps you're right. Although I don't have anything dressy enough to wear with it."

"We'll just have to do some more shopping, then," I said.

Vivienne, seeing that Josephine and I were

taken care of, stood staring at Devi, Maddie, and Glory before disappearing briefly behind a curtain and coming out with a creation a deep rose color with subtle sparkles. She placed it on Glory's head, and I had the sudden memory of when I first met Glory and decided that if she had an aura, it would be precisely this color. With sparkles.

Vivienne took Glory's hand and led her to the mirror.

"Oh, my," Glory said. "How did you know that's my favorite color?"

"Lovey, that's what I do," Vivienne said with a smile as wide as an open door.

She disappeared again and a moment later reappeared carrying two similar hats. One was white shading to pink with a pale pink rose and a darker pink veil. That one she placed on Maddie's head. The second was a peach color with a yellow rose, tinted peach on the tips, and with a darker peach veil. That one she placed on Devi's head. The two young women, at Vivienne's urging, stepped over to the mirror.

Maddie didn't say anything. She just stared.

"Oh, my goodness," Devi said. "You look lovely, Mads."

I've lent Maddie one of my hats for when we go to church together, but it didn't suit her the way this one did. She tipped her head, and then she smiled.

Josephine and I glanced at each other, and Josephine motioned for me to hand her the gift certificate. She then handed it to Vivienne with a wink. Vivienne's hats never have price tags, and I've always suspected she decides what to charge based on how she views the customer.

An unpleasant customer might be quoted a price in the hundreds or even thousands of dollars, at least that's the story going around. But Vivienne has always charged me a reasonable amount.

While Josephine took care of business, I sat watching my friends who looked amazing in their Vivienne originals and, as I do at least once a day, I thanked God for this late-in-life gift of love and friendship.

Chapter Thirty-Two

Josephine

"I could tell yesterday you were plotting about more than buying us all hats, Josephine. So out with it," Lill said when I saw her the next day.

"You know me too well," I said. "And you're right. I am plotting."

"Can you share?"

"Here's the thing. Glory was a sort of whistleblower. Right?"

"I suppose. In a way."

"Okay, maybe not in the strictest sense. But she played a critical role in stopping the Culpeppers and getting some of the victims their money back. And she deserves to be rewarded for that. In my humble opinion."

"Oh, I agree."

"So. I plan to suggest to Richard that some of the JLR trust be used to compensate Glory, at the very least, for her expenses. After all, without her, there'd be no recovered money."

"And you're thinking that might help her have enough to move into Brookside permanently, right?"

"Probably not. But Marge has been looking for an assistant for a while, without any luck."

"Ahh. Of course. Glory would be perfect."

"It does sound like she has the perfect background. And I think Marge will quickly see how advantageous it would also be to have someone like Glory living on site as part of her compensation package."

"Well, if you want to know what I think, I

think it's definitely one of your better ideas," Lill said. "And you do have some good ones. What does Norman think?"

"He's the one who told me Marge needs an assistant."

"I'm worried, though," Lill said.

"Why?"

"I'm afraid this might have been our last adventure. After all, I'm not getting any younger. Besides, there's nothing left for us to investigate."

"Oh, I expect there's always going to be some puzzle for us to solve. How do you feel about digging into Chantelle Winston's naked poker story about her first husband?"

"You thought that was suspicious?"

"Didn't you? It's at least as suspicious as Lottie Watson's story, and look how that turned out."

"But they've moved out."

"Why let a minor detail like that stop us?"

"I suppose we could think about it."

"That's the first step," I said. "And even if there are no more mysteries, we'll have other delights. We get to watch Lily and Toby growing up, and we have our friendships with Devi and Mac and Maddie and Oliver."

"Of course," Lill said, looking a little brighter.

I was glad I'd managed to cheer her up. Now I just needed to work the same magic on myself, because Lill was correct. It seemed our best mystery-solving days are behind us, and I'm going to miss them too.

"Never say never," Norman said when I told him later what I was thinking.

And since he is my major proof that life still has surprises to offer, I repeated his words to myself as he put his arms around me and pulled me close.

I leaned into him, my heart filled with gratitude for the satisfying life we shared, with or without adventures.

About the Author

A former toxicologist and university professor, Ann Warner is the author of a heartwarming cozy mystery series, a romantic trilogy, and six single titles that have collectively garnered over 2,500 five-star reviews. During her career as a clinical toxicologist, Ann encountered many medical mysteries and intriguing stories that have now found their way into her novels.

Ann's cozy mystery series follows the adventures and dodgy events in a not so retiring retirement community. In her trilogy and single titles, the consequences of choosing to love or not to love is an underlying theme. Ann's characters face crises and complications that force them to dig deep within themselves to discover the limits of their own resilience.

Ann lives in Cincinnati, the setting for her cozy mystery series, with her husband. Together they have lived in or traveled to many of the settings found in Ann's books: New Zealand, Australia, Alaska, Colorado, Kansas, Boston, and Puerto Rico.

Hear Ann talk about her writing in the Friday Talk at Ten interview with Joan Bryden, linked on her website.

You can also visit, contact, or follow Ann on the following sites

Website: AnnWarner.net
Facebook: Ann Warner Author of
Emotionally Engaging Fiction

A Note to Readers

Dear Reader,

Thank you so much for the gift of your time in reading *The Babbling Brook Naked Poker Club – Book Six*. I hope you enjoyed it. If you did, I'd very much appreciate it if you would take a moment to tell a friend about the book or to leave a review on Amazon or elsewhere. I am so grateful for reviews. They're vital to my novels' successes.

If you want to keep in touch with me, consider signing up for my mailing list. Signing up is super easy and means you'll receive an occasional newsletter that will include insider information about my writing process and new release notifications. You will also receive a link to a short story as a thank-you for signing up. And don't worry. I hate spam so I won't ever share your address with anyone else!

Thank you!

Acknowledgments

□

Although writing a novel requires solitude, no book gets published in isolation. Of the many people who have contributed to the process for this series, I'm especially thankful to Delores Warner, who provided invaluable expertise to ensure the Graphoanalysis (handwriting) details are correct. Any errors in interpretation or description are mine. Thank you so much, Delores. And thanks to Lynda Dietz who stepped in to edit this book when my regular editor, the wonderful Pam Berehulke, was unavailable.

I also want to acknowledge the tremendous contributions of the members of the Women's Fiction Critique Group on Facebook who were my first readers: Bella Ellwood-Clayton, Jack Bates, Sophie Krich-Brinton, Sarah Hawthorn, Diane Byington, Wendy Norton, Rachael Richey, Gail Cleare, Shannon Evans, Karin Davies, Sara Wegman, Bonnie Ebsen Jackson, Christy Zemudio, and Margaret Johnson. Your insightful comments and suggestions made this a better book.

Inspiration for the Babbling Brook series came, in part, from my experiences as a member of the

Circle Singers, a community chorus. Singing with the chorus at local retirement communities in the Cincinnati area provided me with details that I've used in this series.

To all those who have written to comment on my stories, especially those of you who have told me my novels have been a source of comfort or distraction during tough times, thank you!

My gratitude as well to everyone who has posted a review of one of my books. Your kindness makes it easier for others to discover my novels.

And above all, thanks to my husband, who lights up my life and makes it possible for me to be a full-time writer.

Also by Ann Warner

Dreams for Stones

Book One of the Dreams Trilogy

Available as a free download in multiple formats

Indie Next Generation Book Award Finalist

Electronic, Print, and Audio editions available

☐

A man holding fast to grief and a woman who lets go of love too easily. It will take all the magic of old diaries and a children's story to heal these two. Caught in grief and guilt over his wife's death, English professor Alan Francini is determined never to feel that much pain again. He avoids new relationships and keeps even his best friend at arms' length. His major solace is his family's ranch south of Denver.

☐

Children's book editor Kathy Jamison has learned through a lifetime of separations and a broken engagement that letting go is easier than hanging on. Then she meets Alan, and for once, begins to believe a lasting relationship is possible. But Alan panics and pushes her away into the arms of his best friend. Now the emotions of three people are at stake as they struggle to find a way to transform their broken dreams into a foundation for a more hopeful future.

Persistence of Dreams
Book Two of the Dreams Trilogy
Electronic, Print, and Audio editions available

☐

Lost memories and surprising twists of mystery. Alan, Kathy, and Charles's story continues. The ending of his love affair with Kathy and an arsonist seeking revenge are the catalysts that alter the shape and direction of Charles's life. Forced to find both a new place to live and a way to ease his heartache, Charles finds much more as he reaches out to help his neighbor Luz Montalvo. Helping Luz forces Charles to come to grips with his fractured friendships and the fragmented memories of his childhood.

☐

Luz Montalvo was a carefree college student until her parents died in a car crash. Frantic not to lose her younger siblings to foster care, Luz took them on the run. After nearly a year scraping by as an apartment manager, she's just beginning to feel safe when she discovers her newest tenant is her worst nightmare, a deputy district attorney.

Unexpected Dreams

Book Three in the Dreams Trilogy

Print and Electronic Editions Available

☐

Murder made to look like an accident, family secrets, interfering mothers, lovers in conflict. All combine in a satisfying mix in this contemporary romantic mystery.

☐

Phoebe Whitney-Tolliver has just ended a long-term relationship and begun a new position as the Chief Accident Investigator for the City and County of Denver. She has also fulfilled a lifelong dream—that of owning a horse. These changes bring Phoebe into contact with horse owner and attorney Sam Talbot and Luz and Charles Larimore.

☐

Phoebe helps Charles, a district attorney, and Luz, his wife, in determining whether a traffic accident was actually murder, while Sam locates information about Luz's Chilean family. Eventually the four of them come up against Luz's murderous uncle, a man determined to maintain control of the family's large estancia in Chile. The uncle is a formidable foe, one who will require all the wiles and skill Phoebe, Sam, Charles, and Luz possess to overcome.

Doubtful

Endorsed by Compulsion Reads

Red Ribbon Award - Wishing Shelf Independent Book Awards

Print and Electronic Editions Available

☐

For Dr. Van Peters, Doubtful Sound, on the South Island of New Zealand, is a place to regroup after a false accusation all but ends her scientific career. She is healing and adapting to a simpler lifestyle as she assists a local scientist in his plant studies when journalist David Christianson arrives to disturb her tentative peace.

David has chosen Doubtful as a place of respite after a personal tragedy is followed by an unwelcome notoriety. Neither Van nor David is looking for love or even friendship. Both want only to make it through another day. But when the two are kidnapped and then abandoned in a remote area of the Sound, their only chance of survival will be the courage and resilience with which they face an unforgiving environment.

Absence of Grace

Available as a free download in multiple formats

Print is also available

☐

The memory of an act committed when she was nineteen weaves a dark thread through Clen McClendon's life. It is a darkness Clen ignores until the discovery of her husband's infidelity propels her on a quest for her own redemption and forgiveness. At first, her journeying provides few answers and peace remains elusive. Then Clen makes a decision that is both desperate and random to go to Wrangell, Alaska. There she will meet Gerrum Kirsey and learn that choices are never truly random, and they always have consequences.

Counterpointe

Endorsed by Compulsion Reads

Print and Electronic Editions Available

☐

Art, science, love, and ambition collide as a dancer on the verge of achieving her dreams is badly injured. Afterward, Clare Eliason rushes into a marriage with Rob Chapin. The marriage falters, propelling Clare and Rob on journeys of self-discovery. Rob joins a scientific expedition to

Peru, where he discovers how easy it is to die. Clare's journey, which takes her only a few blocks from the Boston apartment she shared with Rob, is no less profound. During their time apart, each will have a chance to save a life. One will succeed, one will not. Finally, they will face the most difficult quest of all, navigating the space that lies between them.

Love and Other Acts of Courage

Wishing Shelf Independent Book Awards Finalist

Print and Electronic Editions Available

☐

A freighter collides with a yacht and abandons the survivors. A couple is left behind by a dive boat.

☐

These are the dramatic events that force changes in maritime attorney Max Gildea's carefully organized life, where, win, lose, or settle out of court, he gets paid and paid handsomely. As he represents the only survivor of the yacht sinking and gets involved in the search for the couple missing from a dive trip, his reawakening emotions catapult him into the chaos of sorrow and joy that are the necessary ingredients of a life lived fully.

Memory Lessons
Print and Electronic Editions Available

☐

Glenna Girard has passed through the agony and utter darkness of an unimaginable loss. It is only in planning her escape, from her marriage and her current circumstances, that she manages to start moving again, toward a place where she can live in anonymity and atone for the unforgivable mistake she has made.

☐

As she takes tentative steps into the new life she is so carefully shaping, she has no desire to connect with other people. But fate has other ideas, bringing her a family who can benefit from her help if only she will give it. And a man, Jack Ralston, who is everything she needs to live fully again, if Glenna will just let herself see it.

Vocabulary of Light
Print and Electronic Editions Available

☐

Moving to a tropical island might sound like a dream to some people, but for Maggie Chase it's more of a challenge than she's looking for. Maggie, who has a PhD in biochemistry, agreed to put her husband's career first after the birth of their daughters, and that has now led to Mike accepting the position of CEO of the Lillith Pharmaceuticals plant in San Juan. Struggling to fit into the bilingual, Latin culture of Puerto Rico in the late 1980s, Maggie's adjustment is aided by the friendships she develops. Friendships that bring both dark and light into her life, and eventually demand of her an inner strength and resilience she didn't know she was capable of.

Printed in Great Britain
by Amazon

83872075R00185